SMALL
BITES
BACK

Also by Hannah Moffatt

Small!

Shortlisted for the
Waterstones Children's Book
Prize 2023

Praise for *Small!*

'Funny and yucky with characterful caricatures by Rory Walker ... likely to be a hit read aloud. Expect a sequel involving vampires.'   *Sunday Times*, Book of the Week

'A GIANT triumph! Funny, creative and heart-warming. I adored everything from the hilarious giant-school timetables to the swampfish and bogweed sandwiches. And who wouldn't want a best friend like Walloping Toenail? Loved this MG.'   A. F. Steadman, author of *Skandar and the Unicorn Thief*

'Riotous fun.'   Amanda Craig, *New Statesman*

'Vast in humour and heart. A giant of a book.'
                Zillah Bethell, author of *The Shark Caller*

'It's epic. Massive fun, giant amounts of silliness and a huge heart. I loved every page of it.'
                Tom Vaughan, author of *Bin Boy*

'Moffatt tells her tale with comical charm, as the bizarre and bonkers situations ratchet up, bringing ghostly elephants, ballet lessons for the giants and a bad-tempered fairy inspector. Children of eight and up will delight in this gleeful, rambunctious romp.'   *Literary Review*

'It's funny, it's silly and it's simply delightful. Fun with a giant-sized 'F'.'   Rashmi Sirdeshpande, author of
Never Show a T-Rex a Book

'A totally original tall tale that's spurt-your-tea-out funny.'
Lucy Brandt, author of *Leonora Bolt: Secret Inventor*

Praise for *Small Bites Back*

'SMALL BITES BACK is even more hilarious than book 1 (and that's saying something!). The delight of vampire dentists and sinister tooth fairies had me crying with laughter.'   A. F. Steadman, author of
Skandar and the Unicorn Thief

'Riotously funny and inventive.'
Lucy Brandt, author of *Leonora Bolt: Secret Inventor*

'WOW, absolutely fangtastic! Small bites back with a giant bite!'   Zillah Bethell, author of *The Shark Caller*

SMALL
BITES
BACK

**HOW TO DEAL
WITH VAMPIRES,
WEREWOLVES AND
TOOTH FAIRIES**

hannah moffatt

ILLUSTRATED BY RORY WALKER

Published in the UK in 2023 by Everything with Words
Limited, Fifth Floor, 30–31 Furnival Street, London EC4A 1JQ

www.everythingwithwords.com

Printed and bound in Great Britain by
CPI Group (UK) Ltd, Croydon CR0 4YY

A CIP catalogue record for this book is available
from the British Library.

ISBN 978-1-911427-34-6

For Nick – for everything

HM

To my friend, Ste Cammack, 1977–2023

RW

'When zombie clowns gnash their teeth and vampires despair, the Chosen One BITES BACK'

Prediction letter 5274 from the
Fortune Teller in the Cellar

I'm Harvey Small. But you know that already. Don't you?

I'm the one who was always bad news.

Even Mum thought so. That's why she packed me off to Madame Bogbrush's School for Gifted Giants. And I spent the whole term wobbling around on stilts, hoping my classmates wouldn't stomp me into a sandwich!

Then my luck changed.

You see, I'm the one who realised the new spellings teacher, Mistress Ring, was really the evil Ring Mistress from the Unspeakable Circus. She stole Norma Enormous, the school's top clomper, stomper *and* dancer. So I raced through the swamp with my best friend Walloping to save her. Or I tried to. Until I got stuck in a sink pit and Walloping had to save ME.

Now everyone knows I'm not a giant. But it's okay. Madame Bogbrush thinks I'm a hero for helping Norma, so she's let me stay at school.

Oh, and I'm also the *Chosen One*. At least, that's what the school's Fortune Teller in the Cellar says. Everyone thinks this is BRILLIANT ... apart from me.

I thought being bad news was tough.

It turns out being good news is tougher.

Much tougher.

Chapter one

Grave Danger!

It was a normal day at Madame Bogbrush's School for Gifted Giants.

- The swamp was stinking.
- The giants were stomping.
- And Lumbering Turnip …

"… Help! I'm in grave danger!" snivelled Lumbering Turnip.

Lumbering Turnip was in grave danger.

My giant classmate charged across the school field towards me. His face was covered in snot and worry.

I jumped away from Twinkle the skelephant, even

though my undead elephant friend and I were THREE kicks away from a new keepie-uppie record. (Those records were much easier to beat now I wasn't stuck on stilts.)

"*Ruroogha!*" trumpeted Twinkle, flapping her ears.

"Sorry Twinkle," I said. But we couldn't be too careful. I peered around the field, looking for danger. Had the Ring Mistress from the Unspeakable

Circus escaped the Vampire Mountains? (That's where the swamp spat her out last term.) Were zombie lions, or other equally unspeakable circus performers, on the loose?

Had she come back to get us?

"It's my Grunting Theory homework!" moaned Lumbering. "I haven't done it! Madame Bogbrush will stomp me into a sandwich if I don't finish it today! You're the Chosen One, Harvey Small. You have to help me!"

Ah.

This.

Again.

Since the Fortune Teller in the Cellar called me the Chosen One, my classmates are *always* in grave danger. Especially when they haven't done their homework. It turns out I'm not very good at pounding and clobbering, but I'm really good at writing about it.

"You leaves my best friend alone!" said Walloping Toenail, stomping over the field and waggling one of his sausage-sized fingers at Lumbering. "Harvey isn't chosen to do your homework and you knows it!"

Walloping was right.

I just wish I knew what I was chosen for.

What if it was something I'm no good at? Like multiplying fractions.

What if I let everyone down?

What if I let Mum and Dad down? They weren't back together, and I was okay with that. Honest. But they *were* different. Now, when they talked about me on the phone, they didn't argue. Mum didn't sigh or do one of her angry whispers I wasn't supposed to hear. She SMILED. And giggled. Whenever I went anywhere in the school holidays with either of them, they'd introduce me as the Chosen One, and they'd go on and on and on about the fortune teller's prediction to all their friends.

That should make me happy, right?

So why does it feel like there's a small spikey monster living in my tummy blowing raspberries at me?

DING!

DANG!

DUNG!

Dinnertime.

For a moment, the deafening, brain-boggling school

bells clanged louder than my worry. I patted Twinkle's bony back and grabbed Lumbering's homework. "Come on, Lumbering," I said. "I'll help you."

*

Things should have been good.

"Things is so good!" said Walloping, smacking his lips and tucking into one of his favourite swampfish and bogweed sandwiches.

But ever since the Ring Mistress promised something truly unspeakable would happen to me, I've struggled to sleep.

I knew the swamp spat her out.

I knew the Vampire Mountains were a long way from our school, here in the middle of the Stinking Sinking Swamp.

That didn't stop me jumping at every noise. Which meant I jumped all the time as Walloping and the other giants *bashed*, *crashed*, *stomped* and *clattered* everywhere.

"Why does you looks so worried?" said Walloping, scratching his head.

"Yeah," said Norma Enormous. "You should be like me. I'm the best at not worrying." She thudded me on the back so hard my head dunked in a bowl of algae broth. Giant food hadn't improved.

"Oops," said Norma, as I wiped algae from my eyes. "But really Harvey, the Ring Mistress is miles away. She wouldn't be daft enough to steal me again. Not unless she wants Madame Bogbrush to stomp on her."

Our skyscraper-tall Headteacher still *clickety clackety clacked* around the school in meat-pounding high heels. Heels that could flatten us in seconds.

BANG!

And here she was now.

The dining hall door flew open with such force soup splashed out the bowls. The giants jumped to their feet.

Except, it wasn't Madame Bogbrush.

A green light filled the doorway.

We blinked.

Walloping covered his eyes.

The light moved silently towards us, getting bigger and brighter.

It took the shape of two bodies – about the size of grown-up Smalls.

Two *skeleton* bodies.

Each skeleton had a flesh-like green glow flickering over its bones.

One had a wide smile.

The other had an oversized tear stuck halfway down its cheek.

Were they …?

Could they be …?

"**Unspeakable zombie clowns!**" roared every giant in the hall.

I froze.

The unspeakable zombie clowns weren't as terrifying as the description in Walloping's *Big Book for Explorers*.

They were EVEN SCARIER!

Chapter two

More Grave Danger!

Here's one thing to know about giants: they're terrible at hiding.

Some of my classmates covered their

faces with soup bowls. But their ears poked out the sides and gloopy soup splatted everywhere.

SPLAT!

SPLOSH!

SLOSH!

Others ducked under the tables. But their bottoms stuck out, making the tables lift and clonk together.

DONK.

BONK.

THONK.

And even their quietest whispers boomed through the room like they were shouting into megaphones.

"**HIDE!**"

"**SHHH!**"

"**BE QUIET!**"

So I'm pretty sure the two skeleton zombie clowns in the dining hall doorway spotted us.

The smiling zombie clown squeezed a flower-shaped water pistol, shooting a jet of water across the hall. He spoke first.

"Hello boys and girls," he said. His voice squeaked and echoed at the same time. Like a mouse in a tunnel.

We didn't smile back.

"Where is Norma Enormous?" said the sad clown, waving a mouldy custard pie.

A few of the giants shot nervous glances Norma's way. Others looked at me.

Was *this* what I was chosen for? To get rid of the clowns?

I took a deep breath, lowered my soup bowl and put on my best I'm-not-scared-of-zombies voice.

"Norma's not here," I said.

The clowns shrugged and hit each other on the heads with saucepans they'd pulled from their oversized pockets.

"Norma Enormous has signed our Never-Ending Contract," said the smiling one. He clicked his bony fingers and a piece of paper appeared in his glowing green hand. "Norma belongs to the Unspeakable Circus. When our next performance starts in four nights' time, she WILL return. Whether she likes it or not."

A green light snaked from the edge of the contract and across the floor towards Norma. When it reached her, it wrapped around her wrist like a handcuff.

"You don't have a Ring Mistress," I said. "No Ring Mistress, no show." That's how the Unspeakable

Circus works. Walloping had shown me a whole page about it in his *Big Book for Explorers*.

"That's why we're so happy," said the sad clown. "Our Ring Mistress is back!"

I gulped.

This was BAD news. The happy clown giggled, staring straight at me. His eyes flashed green in their sockets. "She has a message for you, Harvey Small," he said. "Or should I say, the Chosen One?"

How did the zombies know about the prediction?

"Our Ring Mistress has chosen YOU to join the circus, too."

The sad clown pulled a string of hankies from a shadowy green sleeve, followed by another sheet of paper.

"Harvey Small, you'll sign this contract and join Norma Enormous in the circus before the moon rises on Friday, OR …" The clown paused.

I held my breath.

The tabletops clonked and soup bowls clattered as the giants shook.

"… OR we'll set our zombie lions on the WHOLE school!"

The sad clown squirted his water pistol flower a second time, soaking half the hall. "And bring our skelephant back, too," he added.

With that, the clowns dropped the contracts and walked away, leaving only a puff of green smoke behind them.

Norma turned whiter than a freshly washed grunting handkerchief.

Could we be in grave danger *again*?

15

Chapter three

Once Bitten

"**D**ANGER! DANGER! ZOMBIE LIONS ARE COMING!" cried the giants. My classmates charged around the hall, grabbing bashing clubs and shouting. They were in such a panic, a few didn't even finish their three-headed worm and cabbage pies. Not in a single bite, anyway.

Norma, Walloping and me stared at the glowing green circus contracts. And at the strange green light that twisted round Norma's wrist.

"Well, I doesn't see why we needs to be scared of a little bit of paper," said Walloping. He snatched my contract away from me.

"It's not the paper that's the problem," I said,

looking at the glowing handcuff of light wrapped around Norma. There was no way I was about to become a zombie performer. And neither was she.

"It's fine. We'll tears up the contracts," said Walloping.

Norma nodded. "Destroy the contracts. Break the light. Good idea. In fact, I was about to say the same thing."

Norma picked up her contract and ripped it in half.

Then she picked up the two halves and ripped them again. And screwed them into balls. And stamped on them. And tossed them into a torch burning on the dining hall wall.

"There, nothing to worry about," she said.

Except …

The torch on the wall fizzled, crackled and shone a bright shade of green.

The giants gasped.

We took a big step away from the flame.

A second later …

Pop!

The paper floated up and out of the torch, landing back on the dining table. It looked good as new.

Norma shook, waved and flapped her arm. Nothing

17

worked. Whatever she did, the green light stuck to her like the stink of old swamp kippers.

"Oh no, oh no, oh no," said Walloping, shaking his head. "Norma, you really has signed a Never-Ending Contract. Those lights aren't normal lights. They is Never-Ending Circus Chains! They is in my *Big Book for Explorers*. You cant's break them." My best friend gave a loud sniff. "You belongs to the Unspeakable Circus now."

That's when Jumbolina shouted, "Quick! Twinkle's in trouble!"

Our classmate stood in the dining hall doorway, waving her bashing club. We raced after her onto the field.

"No!" I cried. A green light, like the one around Norma's wrist, circled Twinkle's middle and snaked into the swamp. She was chained to her contract, too. Wherever it was.

"*Ruroogha!*" said Twinkle, flapping her ears unhappily.

"Don't worry," said Norma, patting Twinkle. "I'll be the best at breaking our Never-Ending Circus Chains. If I put my mind to it."

Norma screwed her contract into a ball and kicked

it into a tree. It smoothed out instantly and floated back to her. She yelled at it, sat on it, and whacked it with her bashing club. But her chains glowed just as brightly.

I took a closer look at the pages. There was something else strange about them. Each one had two jagged holes at the top. "Are those *bite marks*?" I asked.

Walloping gave the contract a long, hard sniff. Then he nibbled the corner. "Yuck!" he said, spitting the paper out again. "It looks like bite marks, but these papers is NOT good enough to eat."

A second later, the contract re-formed, just like before. Walloping's bite disappeared, but the two holes at the top didn't.

They made my brain itch, and the spikey worry monster in my tummy lurch.

Everyone thinks I'm the Chosen One.

I bet a real Chosen One would know a Very Important Clue when they saw it. They'd use that clue to save the day.

"Those bite marks are a clue," I said, standing tall. Unfortunately, without my stilts, standing tall meant my head reached the top of Walloping's kneecaps. I'm not sure he noticed.

"Is they?" said Walloping, peering at the paper.

"I bet …" my brain whirred. "I bet if we find out what bit the contract, we'll find out why it's neverending. Then we'll be able to break it!"

Walloping shook his head. "I isn't sure about that," he said.

"Let's look in your *Big Book for Explorers*, there must be a bit about swamp creature teeth," I said. Maybe, just maybe I could save the school after all!

Walloping and Norma shook their heads. They'd gone pale. They were probably as stunned as me that I'd come up with an answer so quickly. And I had more ideas where that came from.

"Or," I said, "we could talk to a dentist."

Every giant on the field stopped looking at Twinkle and stared at me instead.

Then, they screamed.

Chapter four

Aaaarghhhh!

"AAAAAAAAAAAARRRRRRGGGGGHHHHHHHHHHHHH!!!!!!"

Chapter five

Giants Don't Like Dentists

My ears rang from the screaming. I'd never seen the giants this upset – not even when they found out I was a Small.

"What's wrong?" I asked my whimpering classmates. Being scared of zombie lions who want to chomp your head off made sense. But dentists? I quite liked getting my teeth cleaned. Or at least, I liked getting the sticker afterwards.

"I'm sure a dent— " I began. Before I could finish the word *dentist*, Walloping waggled one of his big sausagey fingers at me.

"We doesn't use that word!" he whispered.

The giants shook their heads and clamped their hands over their mouths.

I wasn't giving up. Those bite marks were our only clue. I waved Norma's Never-Ending Contract at the giants. "Something bit this contract and chained Norma to the Unspeakable Circus," I said. "The bite might have never-ending venom in it. If we spoke to … someone who *knows* about teeth, they could have the antidote. They could help us free Norma and Twinkle!"

My classmates didn't look convinced.

CLICKETY.

At last!

CLACKETY.

Madame Bogbrush marched across the field.

CLACK.

She'd agree with my plan.

Instead of hiding behind Walloping as usual, I ran towards the Headteacher.

"GREAT GOLIATHS! WHAT'S GOING ON HERE?" she snapped. Madame Bogbrush's breath sent me somersaulting backwards into the bushes. The giants mumbled about zombie lions and dentists.

I got to my feet and raced towards her again. I was

24

just close enough for the Headteacher to hear me, when she shouted, "NO. NO. NO! WE ARE NOT LOSING MY MOST GIFTED STUDENT AGAIN. OR OUR CHOSEN ONE."

This time, Madame Bogbrush stopped me flying into the trees by hooking her long fingers

through my dungarees. She dangled me in front of her humungous, frowning face.

"**WELL, CHOSEN ONE … ARE YOU GOING TO FIX THIS?**" she asked.

Something about the Headteacher's saucer-sized eyes made me panic. What if my guess was wrong? What if my plan failed, and Mum and Dad went back to being disappointed in me? And Walloping stopped liking me? And zombie lions ate us all?

What if this was all a terrible idea?

The spikey, raspberry-blowing worry creature in the pit of my stomach started can-can dancing.

"**WELL?**" boomed the Headteacher.

I swallowed hard. It was now or never. I had to *try* and save the school, didn't I?

"Yes," I said, swinging back and forth. "I'll fix this. But I need to talk to a swamp dentist." I took a big risk using the D-word. I hoped the Headteacher wouldn't scream and drop me.

"No!" shouted my classmates.

"It's too dangerous!" said Norma Enormous.

"He'll never make it out alive!" said Lumbering Turnip.

Madame Bogbrush didn't look scared. "**EXCELLENT IDEA,**" she said. "**IT'S A LONG JOURNEY. OGG WILL TAKE YOU FIRST THING IN THE MORNING.**"

Yes! Finally, I wasn't just doing my classmates' homework. I was doing something important. I was saving the school! Probably.

I didn't ask why my friends looked so terrified.

I'd been to dentists before.

How bad could it be?

*

"*I'm tellings you, this is a bad idea. You must finds another way!*" That was the last thing Walloping said before we all went to bed. The next morning, I tried to be cheery.

"Don't worry, Walloping, I'll be back soon!" I said.

"Hmph," he replied, thudding out the dorm to join the others in Clomping class.

I hated fighting with my best friend. But everyone was counting on me. I had to go.

I crossed the field to the school's great golden gates and stared up at Mr Ogg's camper van with monster truck tyres.

Dear Harvey,

How lovely to hear about your school trip to the swamp dentist. Your dad and I are just SO very proud of you. So are the neighbours, and everyone at work. And the bus stop. And the supermarket. And even the man who fixed our leaky loo last Tuesday looked impressed.

Be good, won't you? And open wide when the dentist asks.

Lots of love,

Mum.

Permission Slip

Madame Bogbrush's School for Gifted Giants

I, Mrs Small, give permission for my son, Harvey Small, to go on a school trip to the swamp dentist.*

Signed

Mrs Small

* I promise not to blame the school if swamp goblins attempt to gobble up my son at any point during the trip.

The gates were open, but Mr Ogg wasn't there. Strange.

Teachers were never late. And we didn't have time to waste. The Unspeakable Circus would perform again in three nights! If I didn't save the day (or hand myself over to the circus) by then, the zombie lions would eat us.

At least Twinkle had come to see me off. She nuzzled her shimmery shadow trunk through my hair. "*Rurooogha*," she trumpeted, sadly.

"It's okay, I won't let the Unspeakable Circus take you again," I said, shaking Walloping's words from my head.

I had to save the school … just as soon as Mr Ogg got here.

I waited.

And waited.

And waited some more.

Eventually, Mr Ogg plodded across the field.

PLOD.

PLOD.

PLOD.

The teacher's face was as green as the light from Norma's Never-Ending Contract. (I'd stuffed the bitten pages in the pocket of my dungarees, ready to show the dentist.)

The thought of whizzing through the swamp in Mr Ogg's camper van made my stomach churn. I didn't expect him to feel sick, too.

"**Ogg lost keys. Ogg can't drive,**" he said. But he jangled suspiciously as he walked.

"Are you sure they're not in your pocket?" I asked.

Mr Ogg shook his head and backed away.

"**Nope. No keys. Just noisy pockets. Ogg sick too,**" he said, giving the world's smallest cough. "**Can't drive to d-d-d …**" he squeezed his eyes closed before yelping the word "**dentist**".

He was as scared as my classmates!

Before I could tell him to stop being so silly, he'd run right back into the castle grounds.

"Great," I said under my breath. "What am I going to do now?"

"*Ruroogha!*" trumpeted Twinkle, looking at the open gate.

"*Ruroogha!*" she trumpeted again, kicking her football through it.

"Twinkle!" I cried. "Do you know the way?"

She lowered her shimmery head and bent her knees.

"Oh Twinkle, you're brilliant!" I said, climbing on her bony back. I knew how fast she could tromp through the swamp. We'd reach the dentist and hopefully, maybe, save the school in no time.

Except …

"Wait! Waaaaaaiiiiiiit!" cried Walloping. My best friend charged across the school field, taking giant strides towards us.

My stomach twisted. I didn't want another fight.

"Waaaaaiiiiiit!" shouted Walloping again, getting closer.

Twinkle and I waited, until Walloping was puffing and panting in front of us.

"Harvey Small, you is my best friend," he said. "And if you is facing big danger with the …" the colour drained from his cheeks, "… *dentist* to save us from zombie lions, then I is coming with you!"

He carried a bag that was stuffed full of rolled-up

maps, and by the smell of it, swampfish and bogweed sandwiches.

I grinned. Maybe I didn't have to save the school all by myself.

With Walloping towering by my side and Twinkle carrying me on her back, we set off into the Stinking Sinking Swamp.

For once, I didn't mind the stench.

I didn't feel sick.

Even heckles from the Moaning Marsh didn't bother me.

Ouchy, ouchy eee, stop stepping on meeee!

The circus has won and all you get is this song!

My best friend blew raspberries at the marsh and Twinkle kicked her football right through it. I laughed.

No. The Unspeakable Circus wasn't going to win.

Not this time.

Chapter six

A Grave Warning

Walloping poked his head into his rucksack and sighed. He'd eaten all 27 of the swampfish and bogweed sandwiches he'd packed.

His stomach groaned.

Roaarrrrr!

"Thank goodness we is almost there, I is so hungry!" he said.

All I could see ahead was a massive mountain range. Each peak was higher than the school castle. We didn't look almost there to me.

The sun bobbed down behind the mountains. It made Twinkle's Never-Ending Circus Chains shine even brighter.

"*Ruroogha!*" she trumpeted, flapping her shimmery shadow ears.

"The d-d-dentist be up there," said Walloping, pointing into the mountains. "In The Jaw."

That's when I noticed the rocks ahead were all different shades of white. And surprisingly tooth-shaped.

Strange. I'd only ever heard Walloping talk about one creature that lived in the mountains …

"*Ruroogha!*" trumpeted Twinkle, more loudly this time. She shook her head and squirted swamp dust from her trunk.

"What's wrong?" I asked, leaping off her back. Was she scared of the dentist now, too?

"*Ruroogha!*" The glowing green circus chains around Twinkle's middle shone so brightly I covered my eyes. She flapped and stomped and flicked her tail.

She was edging away from us.

"Twinkle, where is you going?" cried Walloping.

"*Ruroogha!*"

Oh no. "It's those chains!" I said, watching the light twist and tighten around her. "They're dragging Twinkle back to the Unspeakable Circus! Quick! Help me hold her!"

I clung to Twinkle's front leg.

Walloping wrapped his arms around her.

"But the show doesn't start for three nights!" said Walloping, sliding through the sludge. "I can't holds on!" He stumbled to the ground.

I couldn't either.

I landed on top of Walloping.

Oof!

"***Ruroogha!***"

"TWINKLE!" we cried, clinging to each other …

"***Ruroogha!***"

… watching Twinkle's green glow …

"*Ruroogha!*"

… gradually shrink.

"What does we do now?" said Walloping, shaking.

I wanted to run after Twinkle. *Of course* I did. But running wouldn't help us break her Never-Ending Circus Chains. For that, we had to destroy the contract. "We'll come back for you, Twinkle! I promise!" I cried into the swampy darkness.

"Oh no, oh no, oh no," said Walloping, clambering to his feet. "If the circus steals Twinkle, I bet it steals Norma Enormous, too."

He didn't say, "And it's all your fault because you're the Chosen One and you're meant to fix everything," but I was sure that's what he was thinking.

The spikey, raspberry-blowing can-can-dancing worry creature in the pit of my stomach was back. And now it was crashing cymbals.

Two of our best friends were in unspeakable trouble. And if I didn't break the contracts ... or sign one soon ... the whole school was next.

We had to keep going.

We had to climb the mountain.

Walloping bit his lip.

I wanted to show him things would be alright. So, I did what Dad does with me when I'm worried. I helped Walloping picture something he'd like. "Think of all the places you'll see from the top of the mountain! Only a real explorer would climb that high," I said.

A hint of a smile crossed Walloping's worried face.

"You is right! And I is a real explorer!" he said, dashing ahead.

A moment later, he stopped with a *BANG!*

"Ow!" he said, rubbing his knee. "What's this big stone doing here?"

Walloping had bashed into a flat, rectangular stone. It was half-covered by a leafy swamp shrub. I pushed the leaves away for a better look … and shuddered.

"Is that a *gravestone*?" I said. I squinted to read the worn writing engraved on it.

HAPPY FANG DENTAL SURGERY
EVERY MOUTH WELCOME,
EVERY NIGHT OF THE WEEK
(EXCEPT THURSDAYS).
BOOK BEYOND.

"Book beyond? What does that means?" said Walloping, scratching his head.

Beyond the gravestone, the gravelly, icy path wound upwards. "We keep climbing," I said. I put on my best I'm-not-scared-of-the-dentist-or-creepy-mountains smile. I didn't want Walloping to see the gravestone had me spooked.

My best friend stomped ahead. "Oh boy, the higher we climb, the more I sees!" he said.

"Ughh! But what is these swamp bugs?" A swarm of little gold lights whizzed round his head, then shot off down the mountain.

At the same time, my stomach rumbled. I had the strangest urge to eat a big bag of sweets. Extra-sticky ones. But this was no time for eating. Walloping was miles ahead!

"Wait for me!" I panted, struggling to keep up as I skidded over rough patches of icy ground.

Walloping took a few steps back and swung me onto his shoulders. "We'll gets to the top in no time with my giant steps!" he said.

I gripped the straps of Walloping's dungarees and didn't look down. I was used to being as tall as a giant. But being as tall as a Small on a giant's shoulders running up a mountain made my stomach churn.

The higher we climbed, the colder I felt.

My teeth chattered as Walloping knocked snow off every mountain pine tree we passed. Most of it landed on my head.

SPLAT!

SPLAT!

SPLAT!

The ground was getting seriously slippery. I held on tighter, hoping Walloping wouldn't fall.

That's when something else caught my eye.

"Hey what's that?" I said, making Walloping slide to a wobbly halt.

"What's what?" he said, looking around him.

There were some odd letters in the ice in front of us.

!YAWA NUR

"Yawa?" said Walloping, "what's 'Yawa'? And that second word doesn't looks like a word at all!"

"I think it's a reflection," I said, looking around for a hidden sign up in the snowy trees. "The ice is like a mirror. It's reversing the letters."

Walloping scratched his head. "I doesn't know about that. Besides, I wants to do mountain exploring, not reading!"

He kept clomping and clambering upwards, while I looked back, trying to decipher the letters …

Y-A-W-A must be A-W-A-Y.

"It's *AWAY*, the first word's *AWAY*," I said.

"Wowee!" replied Walloping. But he wasn't talking to me. He was gazing out across the top of the mountain. "I thought the world was big! From up here it is so little. Even our school is only as big as my thumb!"

"Er, Walloping?" I said. While my best friend looked over the horizon, I stared at what was RIGHT IN FRONT OF US.

We'd stopped in the middle of a circle of heavy stones.

More gravestones.

1723-1752

VISCOUNT BLOODSUCKER

MASTER OF THE PERFECT BITE

1301-1389

COUNTESS POLISH

SETS A SHINING EXAMPLE

1341-1908

MISTRESS MOLAR

TOOTH AND FANG IDENTIFIER

EXTRAORDINAIRE

1905-1947

COUNT ALGEBRA

COUNTER OF TEETH AND SUPER AT

SUMS

My heart sank. Were all the dentists *dead*? Who was going to help us free our friends from the Never-Ending Circus Chains without them?

"What's wrong?" asked Walloping. "Are you still sure you wants to see the d-d-dentist?" His voice wobbled.

"You know I am," I said. I hoped he wasn't getting the jitters too.

"Okay," he replied, before bellowing, "**HELLO?**

IS ANYBODY HOME?" He was so loud, even the mountains shook.

"**HELLO? IS ANYBODY HOME?**" his voice echoed back.

Then ... silence.

"Maybe the nasty bloodsuckers isn't here!" said Walloping with a shiver. "Maybe we doesn't have to visit them after all! Maybe we cans break the circus chains some other way?"

Wait a minute ...

Happy FANG Dental Surgery?

Weird gravestones?

Bloodsuckers?

Uh oh.

How had it taken me so long to get it?

"Walloping?" I asked. "Are the swamp dentists ... *vampires?*"

Walloping swung me off his shoulders and gawped as if I'd asked if he liked eating swampfish and bogweed sandwiches. "Of course they is, everyone knows that! The Jaw is the real name for the Vampire Mountains!"

So that's why giants were scared of dentists!

I'd worked out the second word in the ice, too. *Run.*

Away. Run.

Somewhere behind the gravestones, I heard the high-pitched whirr of an electric toothbrush. It made the hairs on the back of my neck prickle.

No, not *Away run* …

"Run away, Walloping! Run away!" I cried, hurrying back the way we'd come.

The whirr was getting closer.

Vampire Surveillance Report: #1236

Observations:

Shivering sugar plums! I was doing my usual security shift – keeping the swamp's creatures away from the dentists – when who did I see? A Small and a giant! Wandering up the mountain ... together!

Luckily, they looked as lost as a liquorice torpedo in a bag of popcorn. I'm sure they wouldn't stray so close to a dentist on purpose. (Yuck!)

Still, I took all the usual precautions. I squirted a trail of toffee perfume to lure them back to the swamp. And I scrawled a warning sign on one of the trees, telling them to run.

They're not the sharpest of creatures, but I think they understood my warning. Eventually.

Recommendations:

I'll keep my wings on them, to be sure they get away.

After all our years of work, we can't have creatures suddenly getting their teeth cleaned and ruining our tooth supplies.

Chapter seven

Fangtastic to Meet You!

*W*hizzzzzzzzz. *Wheeeeeeeeeee.*

The high-pitched whirr of the vampire dentist's electric toothbrush was getting louder.

"Eww!" said Walloping, holding his nose. "What's that smell?"

The air had a definite whiff of peppermint. But I wasn't worried about that.

"We can't let the vampires find us!" I said, looking for anywhere to hide on the open mountain top that *wasn't* behind a creepy gravestone.

"I agrees," said Walloping, charging after me. "I doesn't want those nasty d-d-dentists stealing the late-night snacks I hides in my teeth! I has a three-headed

45

worm all curled up to enjoy later!" He smacked his lips.

That was gross, but it wasn't what I was scared of. I'd read loads of books about vampires. One fang in the neck and the Unspeakable Circus would be the least of my worries. I'd be a vampire! Then I'd never be able to go home in case I bit Mum and turned her into a vampire, too. No one would be proud of me then.

We'd barely taken a few steps when the dusky sky went dark. Thick black smoke swirled up from the other side of the mountain. It circled the gravestones and dropped down between us.

Wait, it wasn't smoke. It was bats!

The bats shrieked and cackled.

"Shoo! Shoo!" said Walloping, flapping his arms.

These were no ordinary bats. These bats were carrying a person. A person holding an electric toothbrush.

A vampire dentist!

The dentist had fangs so white, I squinted to see them. He had eyes so green they could have been coloured with crayons. And he had hair so black it was darker than the shadow beneath a giant's stomping boot.

Walloping's knees clonked together. He was shaking.

The vampire's cloak swished behind him. He held the toothbrush in one hand and ran the other through his slick black hair.

"Patients! Patients, at last! Hello! Welcome to Happy Fang Dental Surgery," he said, waving his toothbrush high. It had a bright orange handle, shaped like a carrot. "I'm chief dentist extraordinaire, Viscount Bloodsucker. And it's just *fangtastic* to meet you!"

I squeaked.

The vampire's face fell. He lowered the carrot toothbrush. "Oh," he said. "Didn't you like my little joke? *Fang*tastic." He opened his mouth wide, pointing to his own sparkling fangs. "Get it?"

Walloping whimpered and backed away.

"I've been practising that joke for a thousand and three years. You're my first willing victims. I mean patients! Patients!" said the vampire. He flashed us another perfect smile. "So, open wide and let's see the problem. A wobbly tooth? An infection? Whatever you need, I, Viscount Bloodsucker, the greatest undead swamp dentist, am here to help," he said, skipping between the gravestones.

Walloping shook his head and clamped his mouth shut.

The vampire smiled at me. "If the giant doesn't need help, that only leaves you." He tilted his head and frowned. "Don't be scared, I won't bite ... not while I'm working, anyway," he chuckled.

This was my moment.

The moment where I could step up and do what I was chosen to do.

Or throw up, wet myself and run away.

And I was feeling queasy.

I wanted to run all the way back to giant school and hide under my squeaky bunk bed.

But Norma and Twinkle needed me. And Mum and Dad believed in me.

I took a deep breath and squashed down my TOTAL TERROR.

"Yes," I said. "I need help."

"Splendid!" said the dentist, pulling a pair of blue rubber gloves from inside his cloak and snapping them onto his fingers. "Follow me."

The craggy mountain tops were connected by rickety wooden bridges. The vampire led us over the first one to a smooth marble door.

"Be careful, best friend!" whispered Walloping, following us. The bridge *creaaaaaked* and wobbled under his giant footsteps.

"You joined us at The Cavity," said the vampire, pointing back towards the gravestones. "It's a favourite spot with my apprentices. Did I mention I'm also Headteacher of the swamp's finest dental school: Viscount Bloodsucker's Academy for High-Achieving Vampires? Perhaps you've heard of it?"

I remembered the cloak and fangs Mum and Dad gave me last term. I'd heard of it alright.

The Viscount kept talking. "My students work so hard – counting, polishing and identifying teeth." He looked at his watch. "We must hurry, they're expecting me in assembly at 17.28. Come."

17.28? Why was that familiar?

Of course, I'd seen it on the gravestone outside!

The dentists weren't dead. Well, not completely dead, anyway. The gravestones were a *timetable*! Viscount Bloodsucker was doing assembly at half past five! I relaxed ever so slightly. I bet one of the students could tell me what bit Norma's contract.

The Viscount heaved open the marble door. Gleaming lights hit me.

I'd never seen a room so white or bright. White marble floor. White leather sofas. And a glass coffee table with piles of magazines. The covers had the kinds of stories Dad reads when he thinks no one's watching. Like, *How dusty are YOUR doorknobs? Why everyone's raving about the rotten swamp egg diet*! And *Get the perfect armpits in 3 weeks.*

Walloping ducked to squeeze through the doorway. Rock dust crumbled around him. "It be so small in here!" he moaned. His head brushed the ceiling. He filled half the room.

Viscount Bloodsucker clapped his hands. "Right, let's take a peek at those teeth."

Walloping scooped me up so I hovered above the Viscount's head. "Best friend, no!"

He was right. Being examined by a vampire dentist didn't sound like a good idea.

I pulled Norma's Never-Ending Contract from my pocket, forcing my hand not to shake.

"Viscount Bloodsucker, *this* is what I need help with," I said, waving the bite marks at the vampire as Walloping lowered me again. "The Ring Mistress from the Unspeakable Circus tricked our friend into signing a Never-Ending Contract and now she's chained to the circus! We think a creature with a Never-Ending venom bit the pages," I burbled. "Could you tell us what it was?"

The Viscount scowled.

"Please?" I said.

The Viscount clenched his fists.

"If it's not too much trouble," I added. It's always good to be polite. Even when you're terrified.

The Viscount's rubber gloves must have been warm. A bead of sweat dripped down his cheek. "I don't know a thing about the Unspeakable Circus. Or what my, I mean *its* Ring Mistress is up to." He folded his arms. "She has nothing to do with me. I see swamp goblins for dental check-ups more often than I see her. And do you know how often swamp goblins keep dentist appointments? Never! They never even make appointments!"

Viscount Bloodsucker's cheeks burned red and his eyes flashed green. Had I offended him?

"We don't think you know the Ring Mistress," I said, turning to Walloping. My best friend looked as confused as me. "We just need to know what bit the Never-Ending Contracts so we can … end them."

As I said it, another more worrying thought grew in my mind.

Before moving to the Stinking Sinking Swamp, there was only ONE creature I knew that had a Never-Ending bite. And I was standing in front of it!

The vampire smiled again.

"Yes," he said. "I know precisely what bit this contract."

He leaned closer.

His polished fangs gleamed.

Chapter eight

A Deal with the Dentist

Viscount Bloodsucker moved towards me. And the world moved in slow motion:

- The Viscount's fangs twinkling under the bright reception lights.
- His breath hitting me like a bucketload of ice cubes.
- Walloping's eyes widening in worry.

"Give it here," snapped the vampire, snatching Norma's contract.

He didn't bite me!

I shook more than a 15-tier algae jelly, but I wasn't a vampire! Not yet, at least.

"Well, maybe I don't know *precisely* what bit the contract," murmured Viscount Bloodsucker, peering at the pages. "But I can think of a few culprits. Hairy Maggot-Faced zombies have been known to bite like this." He held the contract up and squinted. "Then again, the double-bottomed pigeon leaves a similar mark. So does the wonky nine-legged spider. Many creatures from the deepest, darkest corners of the swamp are known for their vicious venom."

I let out the breath I'd been holding.

I'd got vampires all wrong.

They didn't want to bite us, they wanted to help us!

"BUT," said the vampire, thrusting the glowing green contract back at me, "Why should I help you?"

Oh.

"Because we is in trouble!" said Walloping. He rushed to my side and knocked the reception's glass coffee table, sending its fancy magazines flying.

The Viscount winced at the mess. "Perhaps you should have thought about that before turning down my many invitations. Every year we invite your most gifted students to study with us. You never do. Every year we invite you to admire our toothbrush collections. Not a single swamp creature comes."

Was that a tear he was wiping from his eye?

"And when have you ever asked us to watch a single grunting display? Or to polish your teeth?" Walloping yelped and covered his mouth.

"Never! That's when," said the vampire. "So, since you aren't here for a check-up, you can leave."

"Good idea!" said Walloping, pulling me towards the door.

A giant-sized bit of me wanted to run away too. But if I did that, I knew I'd let my classmates down.

Besides, I had an idea.

"Oh, Viscount Bloodsucker, I completely forgot to tell you …" I began, slapping my palm to my forehead. "We're Madame Bogbrush's second and third most gifted students," I fibbed. "Madame Bogbrush sent us here because we really, really, really want to study in your school."

"No, we doesn't!" said Walloping, frowning.

"Shh!" I elbowed my best friend's knee.

"I'm so silly, I should have told you that first," I babbled. "We want to be swamp dentists, like you!"

"I doesn't!" said Walloping.

I jabbed him again.

"Then maybe, if it's okay with you, we can learn about Never-Ending bites and chains and save our friends at the same time."

The vampire arched an eyebrow.

"Isn't that RIGHT, Walloping?" I said, turning to my best friend and mouthing a big "YES".

"Er, yes?" he said. He'd have been more convincing if he wasn't shaking his head.

"Hmm," said the vampire, looking us up and down.

A moment later, he clapped his hands.

"Of course, this is a bloodsuckingly brilliant idea! It's the school photo shoot on Friday. A giant and a Small could be just what we need!" He made L-shapes with his fingers, creating a frame and moving it towards us at different angles.

"Yes! With your smiles in the shot, swamp creatures great, small and slimy will see there's no need to be scared of the dentist! They'll be queuing up to visit Happy Fang Dental Surgery!"

I thought back to the field full of screaming giants when I said the word "dentist". Getting any of them to go near a vampire would be HARD.

"We'll make posters and banners and postcards!" the vampire went on. "We'll share them with everyone! Do this for me and you can study here."

"We can?" I said, my heart lifted. "Thank you!" Even Walloping gave a confused grin.

"Yes!" said the Viscount, prancing through Walloping's legs and around the reception. "Until the photographer comes in three nights' time, you can work with my apprentices! I'll make finding that tooth a special project!"

Three nights.

In three nights, the Unspeakable Circus would perform again. And the Ring Mistress would set her zombie lions on the school.

Would we break the circus chains in time?

"Just remember," said the Viscount, looking serious, "There's only one place in the swamp where you'll find that tooth. And it's right here in my school. I can't have my apprentices roaming outside and getting lost. Understood?"

I nodded, relieved we were in the right place. Everything was going to be okay.

"Tidy up your appearance before the photo, though," said the vampire. His eyes shot to the only corner of the room that looked less than perfect: a large empty space on the side wall. It had a faint grey outline, like something should have been hanging there.

The Viscount caught me staring.

"Sorry, force of habit," he said. "The Narcissus has only been missing a thousand years."

"The Narcissus?" I asked.

"The largest mirror in the whole swamp," he sighed. "We're better off without it. Us vampires found admiring our reflections all day did us no good. Our undead beauty is distracting." He smoothed his cloak and pushed his shoulders back. "We lost days staring at ourselves when we weren't careful. It wasn't even the real us! Everyone knows mirrors reverse your image. Yet still, we were transfixed."

The vampire tilted his head, put his hands on his hips and pouted.

"What's he doing?" whispered Walloping

"I think he's posing," I replied. He looked just like the cover model on the *Vampire About Town* magazine Walloping had knocked off the coffee table.

Viscount Bloodsucker stood perfectly still; eyes glazed over, not saying a word.

"Is he asleeps?" whispered Walloping.

I wasn't sure, but I hoped he wouldn't stay like that for long. We were in a hurry!

Eventually a gong chimed deep in the mountain.

DONGGGGGGG!

The vampire blinked. For a second, he looked surprised to see us. Then he smoothed his perfect hair again and smiled. "Do we have a deal?"

I ran a hand through my own hair, pulling out stray pine needles and twigs.

The vampire's face twisted. I guessed we didn't bring the glamour to the school photo he was hoping for. Before Viscount Bloodsucker could change his mind, I held out my hand.

"Deal," I replied.

"Splendid!" said the vampire. "Then welcome to

Viscount Bloodsucker's Academy for High-Achieving Vampires."

Chapter nine

BITE!

My old first-day-at-school nerves tangled inside my stomach.

Viscount Bloodsucker led us down a dark, narrow corridor. Walloping edged sideways to fit. "Ugh, this mountain is too small!" he moaned.

"You'll need these," said Viscount Bloodsucker,

thrusting small blue torches into our palms. Well, a normal-sized torch for me. Walloping's was no bigger than a toothpick. I wondered if mountains had a lot of power cuts.

The corridor opened onto an auditorium, with rows of seats.

Walloping yelped and I swallowed hard.

There were *hundreds* of vampires here! They were all sitting quietly, backs straight, hair straight, and (I was willing to guess) teeth straight. I stood straighter, too. Walloping picked his nose.

Then the vampires saw us.

And the whole place erupted.

"Patients! We have patients! At last!" they cried. "We always knew this night would come!"

The vampires surged towards us.

"I want to examine them first!"

"No, me!"

"Meee!"

Walloping turned as white as a vampire dentist's perfectly polished fangs.

"Is it true giants never brush their teeth?" said one vampire, bouncing around Walloping's knees.

"Stop it, Gargle!" said Viscount Bloodsucker.

"Can we smell your breath?" said another. She waved a contraption that looked like a giant thermometer.

"Floss! Put that away," said Viscount Bloodsucker.

"What's that?" whimpered Walloping. As his breath hit the contraption, a blue light flashed, alarms went off … and piles of breath mints rained down from the ceiling.

"Emergency mints! Hurry, eat them all," said Floss, holding her nose.

Only one vampire stayed exactly where she was. She let

out a long, loud sigh. "They're not patients," she said. "Look at them, they're terrified."

The other vampires hissed at her.

"Yes, young Clot!" said Viscount Bloodsucker. "Walloping Toenail and Harvey Small are something *even better* than patients. They're here to star in our school photo shoot! I mean photo!"

Everyone *ooohhhhed*. Apart from Clot. Clot yawned.

"But Viscount Bloodsucker ..." I began. He needed to tell the vampires about the tooth we were looking for, not the photo!

The Viscount turned his back to me. "To celebrate," he continued, "is everyone ready to BITE?"

"Eek!" I squeaked. I jumped so high I landed in Walloping's arms. The school rules were on the wall. They said, "No biting!"

"On my count, apprentices, one, two, three ... BITE!" shouted the Viscount.

And something strange happened.

All at once, the vampires hopped on one leg.

They twirled three times.

They gnashed their fangs.

And they shone their blue torches on the ceiling, casting toothbrush-shaped shadows.

Then they looked at us.

"Go on. We're waiting," said Viscount Bloodsucker.

The apprentices stared.

"Waiting for what?" asked Walloping.

"BITE! BITE! BITE!" cheered the vampires.

I took my torch and waved it around a bit.

"No," said Viscount Bloodsucker. "Do it properly. With *all* the moves. There's no sense of occasion if you don't do all the moves." He pointed to a sign hanging beside the school rules.

Viscount Bloodsucker's Academy for High-Achieving Vampires

The BRUSHER IN TOOTH EMERGENCY (BITE) Signal

Any vampire dentist's apprentice who spots a brusher in need of immediate dental assistance should attract attention by:

1. Hopping on one leg
2. Twirling in a circle
3. Gnashing their teeth
4. Flashing their toothbrush torch in the air

Make this signal and the vampire dentists solemnly swear to come to your immediate aid.

Clot rolled her eyes. "I don't know why we bother," she said. "Nobody even knows if the BITE signal works. Since no swamp creatures want to see us, we've never tried it. No one cares about us. All alone in The Jaw …" Her voice made me feel sad. Like opening the biscuit tin to find someone's scoffed the last one.

"Of course it works! It's an unmissable signal!" said Viscount Bloodsucker. He turned back to us. "Off you go …"

We tried our best, we really did.

But the second my best friend hopped, rock dust crumbled into the vampires' perfect hair.

Twirling was worse. I crashed into the Viscount and a dizzy Walloping tumbled into the vampires in the front row.

Viscount Bloodsucker held his hands up. "That's enough practice after all!"

"But we hasn't flashed our torches yet!" said Walloping, shining his tiny torch straight at the Headteacher.

"Never mind," said the Viscount, glancing at an ornate gold clock on the back wall. It was just gone 6pm. "It's 18.01. Time for my apprentices to join Countess Polish."

Hmm. Wasn't it a bit late for lessons?

Seeing me frown, the Viscount said, "You wanted to study here. You must have known this is a *night* school. Our delicate complexions don't do well in the sun. Even when we're inside a mountain."

I stifled a yawn.

"Will Countess Polish help with our project?" I asked. I was tired, but not too tired to find that tooth.

"Oh no," said Viscount Bloodsucker. "You'll need a very special vampire to help with that."

"I'll help the giant!" cried Gargle!

Walloping grabbed my hand so hard I winced. "I is staying with you!" he whispered.

"And I'll help the Small!" said Floss.

The other vampires waved and begged Viscount Bloodsucker to pick them instead. All of them apart from …

"Clot!" said Viscount Bloodsucker. "Our new apprentices will work with you. It'll be a good chance to improve those dismal grades of yours. I expect YOU to take good care of our guests."

Clot stood up and sloped towards us. As she got closer, I saw a small black and orange bat was curled round her wrist and snoozing.

68

"Look! Look! Look!" said Walloping, jabbing me in the side so hard I fell into the Viscount. "I meets another swamp creature!"

Clot peered up at Walloping, then moved her arm with the bat behind her back.

"Aw, fiddle clubs!" said Walloping, leaning over Clot's head to get a look at the bat anyway.

The Viscount handed Clot an exercise book with *Very Important Tooth-Finding Project* scrawled across the front. He murmured a series of instructions in her ear.

Clot scowled.

And shrugged.

And rolled her eyes.

And my hopes of finding the tooth we needed fast, fizzled away.

"Come on. Let's get it over with," she said, barely looking at us. Clot trudged down the corridor to a plain stone door.

She heaved it open.

And you'll never guess what was inside.

Chapter ten

A Taste for Blood

Teeth.

I'd never seen so many teeth.

Yellowing, gnarly old teeth.

Teeth piled up on desks.

Teeth teetering on shelves.

Teeth crashing over us
into the corridor
like a very
pointy
wave.

Can you drown in teeth?

I hoped not.

"Aghhh!" said Walloping, leaping back. "I doesn't like it here!"

"What did you expect?" sighed Clot. The bat snoozing on her wrist wriggled. It was so late, I wished we were snoozing, too.

"You're looking for a tooth, aren't you?" said Clot. "Which means *I'm* looking for a tooth. I can't fail my beginner's dentistry exam again, so you'd better not mess this up for me."

My insides crumbled more than the crumbliest apple crumble. Viscount Bloodsucker had said he'd help. But searching through all these teeth could take days. And he hadn't exactly picked the school's best student to help.

I laid Norma's contract out on the floor. Clot picked up one small tooth and jabbed it at the bite marks.

It was too small.

"Nope," she said, tossing the tooth right back into the pile.

She did the same thing with a second tooth, then a third.

"Ooh! Algae pies!" said Walloping, sniffing one of the larger teeth. "I think that's what the creature who loses this tooth eats for their dinner." My stomach churned at the thought.

When his tooth didn't fit, Walloping copied Clot and threw it back in the pile.

We needed a better system.

I pushed the teeth that were clearly too big (some were bigger than my whole head!) to one side.

"*Mmmm*!" said Walloping as he sniffed and then LICKED a jagged brown tooth. Something green dribbled down it. "Ooh, this creature had bogweed and fungus pancakes for breakfast, yum! When is we eating?"

My stomach churned some more. The last thing I wanted to do was eat. Especially with Clot staring at me.

I didn't know much about vampires. But if a vampire licks their lips as they look at you, that can't be a good thing, can it?

"We're not hungry!" I said hurriedly. I grabbed another tooth and pretended to concentrate extra hard as I placed it in the bite marks.

"Yes we is! We is tired and hungry and we hasn't

even had dinners!" said Walloping, folding his arms. "And you says to me you is hungry, too!"

I pretended not to hear my best friend – even though inside this mountain, his voice bounced and boomed off the walls, making toothbrushes, toothpicks and tiny mirrors on sticks fly off the shelves.

I had to play it cool.

I picked up one of the mirrors and pretended to use it to examine a tooth.

Clot flinched. Then, she laughed. Not a warm, Walloping kind of laugh. This was like a slap in the face from a damp sock.

She peered up at Walloping and pointed at me with a toothpick. "Your friend here thinks that because I'm a vampire, and because he's so human and *juicy*, that I'll want to drink HIS blood for breakfast."

I gulped hard. My worry sounded even worse when Clot said it out loud!

I backed away as far as I could, stumbling over stray teeth.

The corners of Clot's mouth flickered upwards, like she wanted to smile but couldn't remember how. "He doesn't know we're vegetarian," she said.

"What?" I said, shaking my head. Maybe this was a

sneaky vampire trick to make sucking my blood even easier. "Vampires drink blood, everyone knows that!" I blurted.

Coming here had been a terrible mistake.

We had to escape!

Before I could run, Clot pulled something from inside her cloak and launched it at me.

"Eek!" I cried, ducking just in time. The vampire was trying to knock me out!

"Ooh, an orange!" said Walloping, unhelpfully.

"Walloping, will you STOP licking teeth and RUN!" I cried.

My best friend's eyes widened and watered.

When I noticed what he was holding, a pang of guilt bopped me on the nose.

"Hang on … Is that an *actual orange*?" I asked, staring into my best friend's hand. I was confused.

Clot gave her biggest sigh yet. "Yes, it's an *actual orange*. I was giving your friend a snack," she said. "Vampires don't suck blood, we suck blood *oranges*. The extra tangy ones. Bit of a guilty pleasure. Viscount Bloodsucker thinks too many oranges are bad for the teeth. Even though legend says he once sucked the juice from 250 oranges in ten minutes!"

Clot gave another almost-smile. "That's how he got his name."

I'd been gripping my mirror on a stick this whole time. Now I giggled with relief and dropped it in my pocket. We'd probably need all the tools we could find to identify that tooth.

Walloping grinned and gobbled the orange whole, peel and all. "Thanks!" he said.

"It's just an orange. Your giant moaning was hurting my ears," muttered Clot.

She picked up another tooth. This time, when it didn't fit, I caught it and gave it to Walloping.

We didn't talk much after that. But, together, we measured the teeth, ordered them in groups and Walloping piled up the ones that didn't fit in his humungous hands.

Even through Clot's sighs and my sleepiness, I felt a flicker of hope. Maybe we'd find that tooth tonight.

Hours later, a gong chimed again from somewhere deep in the mountain.

DONGGGGGGGGG!

And Viscount Bloodsucker swept down the corridor towards us.

"We've nearly checked every tooth," I said. "But we

can't find the one we're looking for." The Headteacher had told us we'd find all the answers in his school, so I was sure he'd know what to do.

"Well done my apprentices, well done! Why you've made excellent progress!" he said. "Unexpectedly excellent progress," he added under his breath. Instead of smiling, his brow knitted in a frown. "It's been a long night, you must be ever so tired." Then the Viscount stretched his arms high and gave a huge yawn.

It wasn't any old yawn.

It was a yawn so wiiiiiiiiiiiiiiiiiiiiiiiiiiiiide and so **LOUD** you couldn't see it or hear it without yawning too.

Which was fine for me but …

"WALLOPING! NO!" I cried as my best friend stretched his arms high, wiggled his fingers and dropped every single tooth we'd tested on the floor!

"Oops!" said Walloping.

Clot fell to her knees, trying to put the teeth back into piles. And the bat on her wrist woke with a start and a *squeak* and flapped round our heads in circles.

"Shh, Fruity, shh," said Clot, calling after the little bat.

"Oh, deary me!" said the Viscount, looking much happier. "You'll just have to retest ALL these teeth tomorrow. Never mind. It will keep you busy until the photographer arrives. Come now. Bed!"

Hmm.

I couldn't help thinking Viscount Bloodsucker had yawned like that on purpose.

Maybe he wasn't being as helpful as I thought.

Maybe he didn't want us to find that tooth at all.

Apprentice name: Clot
Project: Fang Finding
Night: one
Equipment:
- weird piece of paper with glowing green bite mark
- one giant
- one Small
- one magnifying glass
- all the teeth in the entire school

Oh joy. A special project just for me. Sifting through every single tooth the vampires have ever collected to find one that matches perfectly with this bite mark. Darkness knows how long that will take. My "partners" say they're in a hurry. But the giant knocks or breaks everything he touches. And I don't like the way the Small waves our tools around. I nearly saw myself in a mouth mirror earlier! I don't have time to get lost in my reflection and fail another year of exams. Not again.

I am a lone vampire. Partners only make projects harder.

Still, there's something weird about that green light coming right off the page. What does it remind me of?

Maybe if I paid more attention in lessons, I'd remember...

Teeth examined: 127
Teeth accidentally dropped: 127
Matches: 0

Patience, young Clot! Don't go worrying your undead head about glowing green lights. They have NOTHING to do with this project. Check the teeth again more carefully. The right one can only be in that room. I should know, I'm the Headteacher. VB

Chapter eleven

The Sleep of the Dead

I was so tired when Walloping and me stumbled into the vampires' dorm rooms, I almost didn't notice how TOTALLY CREEPY they were.

Almost. It's pretty impossible to miss row after row of reclined dentist's chairs with GRAVESTONES at the end of them. Especially when one had my name on it.

Here Lies Harvey Small. May He Rest in Peace.

I stared at the stone and shuddered.

The beds didn't bother Walloping. "Oh boy, I is so sleepy! And I has always wanted to try the Sleep of the Dead!" he said, jumping straight onto the chair.

I held my breath, waiting for a *creak* to become a *twang* and most likely a *bang*.

When it didn't (I guess vampires really did want to welcome all creatures. Even giants), I dared to ask, "The Sleep of the Dead? What's that?"

"Oh, you'll sees!" Walloping beamed, reaching his arms out in such a wide stretch he accidentally bopped the vampires either side of him on the ears.

Instead of getting cross, the vampire apprentices sat bolt upright in their beds and started chattering.

"How's the project?"

"Did you find the rare fang?"

"Why are you working with Clot? She's hopeless! You should work with us."

"You'll never find a rare fang in that classroom you know, that's not where we keep the best teeth!"

Every student spoke at once and over the top of the others.

"Slow down!" I said – their voices made my sleepy head spin. I had to focus, especially if they knew something Clot and Viscount Bloodsucker didn't.

"Where should we look for the best teeth?" I asked.

Deep inside the mountain the gong donged six.

*DONG. DONG. DONG. DONG. DONG.
DONG.*

And without answering, every single vampire crossed their arms over their chests, toppled back onto their beds, closed their eyes and fell fast asleep.

"Awww," said Walloping, rubbing his own eyes. "I guess the Sleep of the Dead only works on vampires. They'll be like that all day now. Nothing can wake them."

I nudged them and prodded them and said over and over, "Where do you keep the best teeth?" No reply.

"Walloping, do you think we're looking in the wrong place?"

My best friend would have an answer.

"Walloping?" I said again.

Snurgklehurglepfffft … parp!

The only noise he made was a roaring snore.

Maybe the Sleep of the Dead worked on giants after all.

*

The next night's search didn't start well. Walloping

refused to do anything before breakfast. But a vampire's breakfast wasn't like a giant's one.

"Is this all there is to eats?" said Walloping with a sniff.

Rows of vampires sat on grey benches and sank their heads fangs-first into slices of blood orange. Beside each orange was a glass of milk, a small slice of cheese and a little paper cup filled with bright blue mouthwash.

The apprentices cooed and waved when they spotted us.

"Sit here!" said Gargle, bouncing up and down.

"No! There's space with me!" said Floss, pushing another vampire off the bench to make room. "I'll help with your project!"

I smiled and waved and walked towards her. Help, at last!

Before I could ask a single question, Clot was beside us, scowling.

"No, this is MY project, and we DON'T need help!" she said. "I'll lose marks."

Saving our friends was more important than Clot's grades. Still, I hesitated, turning to my best friend. "Walloping, do you think we should get extra help?"

"Where's the rest of the food?" said Walloping, holding the orange peel between his thumb and finger. "And why is this drink blue? Nothing natural in the swamp is blue!" he complained, accidentally crushing the paper cup of mouthwash in his hand.

Floss and Gargle beamed and sprang on top of the table, paper cups in hand. "It's blue, so we can do this," they said, waving to the other vampires to join them.

"Ughh, not this again," said Clot, rolling her eyes.

"A one, two, a one to three, four," cried Gargle, tapping his foot on the table and clapping his hands. A second later, all the vampires were on their feet (feet which were wearing bright yellow wellies). They all

gargled in time – spluttering and gurgling a tune that sounded just like *Happy Birthday to You*.

The tune was good but …

Kersploosh!

… I covered my eyes as blue spit shot straight at them.

Walloping stared agog. "They're spitting it out!" he cried. The vampires shot jets of mouthwash across the hall, splattering it back into the little paper cups. The spit swirled and flew like a fancy fountain outside Smallington Palace.

Walloping's cheeks turned pink. "Giants never spit out food!"

"They're showing off, ignore them," said Clot, sighing. "They've always wanted someone to watch their gargling displays. Come on, we've got work to do." She plodded out the dining hall. Fruity, the little black and orange bat, flapped after her. We followed, too.

"Wait!" Floss called. "Do you want to borrow our wellies? You haven't heard our best song, yet!"

After the apprentices' warnings last night, I didn't think the tooth we needed was in the classroom. I was going to say something, but before we'd even opened the door, Viscount Bloodsucker swept in front of us.

"Apprentices, where are you going? It's Thursday. Hair dye night. You want to look your best for the photograph, don't you?" The teacher held out two bottles of dye.

I *wanted* to save our friends from the Unspeakable Circus.

"Can we dye our hair *after* we've found the tooth?" I asked. If I could prove the tooth wasn't in the classroom, the Viscount would have to help us find it somewhere else.

The vampire clapped his hands. "What a wonderful attitude to classwork. Young Clot could learn a thing or two from you."

Clot sighed. Fruity clicked her tongue and flapped.

"But no. You can dye your hair *after* posing practice. The photographer will be here tomorrow. I have a feeling in my fangs we must practise our smiles some more. I want them to be *extra* welcoming this year."

Walloping already had one of the friendliest smiles around. He didn't need extra practice.

The Headteacher clapped his hands. "Come now,

follow me outside to The Cavity. Your classmates are waiting."

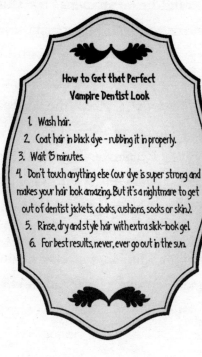

**How to Get that Perfect
Vampire Dentist Look**

1. Wash hair.
2. Coat hair in black dye – rubbing it in properly.
3. Wait 15 minutes.
4. Don't touch anything else (our dye is super strong and makes your hair look amazing. But it's a nightmare to get out of dentist jackets, cloaks, cushions, socks or skin).
5. Rinse, dry and style hair with extra slick-look gel.
6. For best results, never, ever go out in the sun.

HAIR DYE
FOR VAMPIRES

"Aww, we is never going to finds that tooth," said Walloping, shaking his head. He was disappointed in me, I could tell.

I was disappointed in me, too.

I felt sick.

Still, we followed the rest of the

class and gathered on top of the mountain, standing between the gravestones.

"Okay, my beautiful, brainy students," said Viscount Bloodsucker. "Let me see your biggest and brightest smiles!"

"Eek!" squealed Walloping, leaping behind me. "Why is the vampires looking at me like that?"

Whatever the apprentices were doing, it wasn't smiling. Their mouths twisted as they opened them, and their arms (that were meant to be wide and welcoming) looked like they might strangle us at any moment.

Some held shiny toothpicks which flashed in the moonlight, making them look as sharp as the students' highly polished fangs. No wonder they scared the swamp creatures.

Clot didn't even attempt to smile. She stood in the darkness and scowled.

And then … "Ouch!" she cried, rubbing her arm.

A swarm of golden lights buzzed around us, blew raspberries, and shot back down the mountain, leaving only a whiff of marshmallows behind them.

They were just like the bugs that flapped round Walloping when we first climbed the mountain.

"What was that?" I asked Clot.

"Ugh, just the tooth fairies," she said. "They don't like us because we borrow a few of their teeth for our studies. When they see us, they bite us … with their teeth and the ones they steal."

I raised an eyebrow. Most creatures *wanted* tooth fairies to take their teeth. It was vampires that stole them. But it gave me an idea.

If we couldn't find the tooth we needed in Viscount Bloodsucker's school, there was another place we could try.

"Walloping!" I said. "We've got to follow those fairies!"

Vampire Surveillance Report: #1237

Tooth Fairy: Bonnie Bonbon

Observations:

Shake my lollipops! My warning didn't work! The Small and the giant visited the dentist.

I know the Fairy Queen will want to strip my tooth fairy security badge for this. But, I have good news. The giant's breath still pongs like boiled kipper and swamp cabbage surprise. No sign, I repeat NO SIGN of any tooth polishing.

Now the Small and the giant are ON THE MOVE.

Recommendations:

Guide them to the Fairy Queen. One lick of her new double cherry, fizzy whizzy extra lovely lollipop and they'll forget they even saw the dentist. Failing that, we'll stick their teeth together with toffee until they promise not to talk. The last thing we need is swamp creatures saying dentists aren't scary.

Never fear. We'll have this whole mess sorted before you can say Bonnie Bonbon likes a Sherbet Dibdab.

Chapter twelve

Follow those Fairies!

Walloping and I were dashing down the gravel path after the tooth fairies, when Clot grabbed my arm. "Where do you think you're going?" she said. "We've got a project to do!" I guessed Clot wouldn't like our plan. Clot didn't like much of anything we said.

"We searched the entire school tooth collection yesterday and we didn't find a single one that could have bitten the Never-Ending Contracts," I said. "Following the tooth fairies might be our only chance to save our friends." Clot folded her arms. "It could help you pass your project, too," I added.

"Viscount Bloodsucker told you to stay in school.

He said we'd find the tooth here. What if leaving is cheating and I fail my exams all over again because of you?" Clot's face turned greyer than a storm cloud. "Anyway, you can't go now. It'll be dawn in a few hours. You know what happens at dawn."

"No. What happens?" I said, staring at her blankly.

"You *burn*," she whispered. Her eyes were wider than Walloping's.

I was pretty sure Walloping and me wouldn't burn. We were always out at daytime. But Clot? I'd heard stories about vampires burning in the sun. I guess they were true.

"It's okay, we're not asking you to come with us," I said. "We'll find the fairies while the class are busy posing and dying their hair for the photo. We'll be back before Viscount Bloodsucker knows we're gone." Even as I said it, I wondered if we'd get away with it. The teacher *had* asked us to stay put.

Clot gave her longest, grumpiest sigh yet.

"Fine, if you insist, I'll take you. As long as we're quick," she said.

"No, we're not asking …" I began, before Clot carried on.

"We've just got to get Fruity from the roost first,"

she said, heading away from the tooth fairies and towards one of the bridges between the mountain tops. Walloping and I exchanged confused glances. Had we asked her to come?

"The roost?" I asked, following her.

"It's where Fruity sleeps when she's not with me. I wasn't having her posing for that pointless photo. But I don't go anywhere in the swamp without her."

Walloping clapped his hands. "Good idea! And maybe I cans play with him this time!" Walloping had been looking longingly at that little bat ever since we arrived.

"Clot, we don't want you to get in trouble," I tried again.

Clot acted like I hadn't said anything.

She led us across the next mountain peak, towards a rickety wooden barn. She'd barely opened the door before a blur of orange and black shot out and flapped round her head in circles.

"I know, Fruity," said Clot. "I'm happy to see you, too."

When she talked to her bat, Clot didn't look like her grumpy self at all. She sounded almost ... happy. Maybe having her along wouldn't be so bad.

Walloping rushed towards Fruity holding his huge arms out wide. "Hello again, little fella!" he grinned.

Fruity squawked and shook behind Clot's shoulder.

Walloping's face fell. "Aw, I isn't gonna hurts you, boy," he said, giving Fruity a dribbly grin.

"She's a girl, actually," said Clot, her usual coolness returning. "And she's got a great sense of direction. Knows exactly how to get through the swamp in the dark."

"She is so funny-looking!" said Walloping, pointing at the fuzzy orange band around the bat's neck.

"No, you're funny-looking, giant," said Clot, before turning and trudging down the mountain.

Walloping and I hesitated, watching her go.

I shrugged. "I suppose we should follow her," I said, not feeling entirely sure.

It was a long walk.

Even though Clot was about my size, her steps were as heavy as Walloping's.

STEP.

SIGH.

STEP.

SIGH.

The air lost its minty freshness, but it was cool and the full moon was bright.

"Which way now?" I asked when we reached the bottom.

"I hears Extra Smalls – that's fairies – live in marsh marigolds!" said Walloping. "It's in my *Big Book for Explorers*!"

Fruity clicked her tongue, loop the looped and shot off in front of us.

"That's right," said Clot, pointing after Fruity. "Tooth fairies live in rare white marigolds. Past the Moaning Marsh, over the Stinking Sink Pits, behind the Werewolf Den and just beyond the Deadly Creature-Eating Plants. It's a long walk, so no dawdling," she said.

"Boy oh boy, I does so much exploring!" said Walloping, bounding past her.

I jogged to keep up. But I didn't like the sound of our route.

"Deadly Creature-Eating Plants?" I puffed, running into the swamp. "Isn't there another way to get there?"

"Oh no," said Clot, brightening. "You've *got* to see them. They've got the sharpest teeth in the whole swamp."

I didn't want to be eaten by a plant – *especially* not by a plant with extra-sharp teeth!

"So, is that why you're coming with us?" I asked. "To examine plant teeth?" Since Clot clearly didn't like us, I couldn't understand why she'd risk trouble to help now.

"You might be surprised to hear I *don't* want Happy Fang's first-ever visitors to die horribly when Viscount Bloodsucker asked *me* to look after you," she said.

Yes, that surprised me.

"If you don't make it back to that school of yours, everyone will say it's our fault. Vampire dentists always get blamed for things. It's hard enough living one lifetime where nobody likes you. Imagine what it's like living forever."

Clot's bottom lip trembled and she turned away from me. Fruity landed on her shoulder and squawked at us.

"*We* like you, don't we Walloping?" I said.

"I, er, maybe. When you is being nice and giving me oranges and not rolling your eyes," said Walloping.

Clot rolled her eyes.

"Anyway," she said standing straighter, "I always fail Tooth Fairy Taming, I need the practice." She pulled a battered old book out of her cloak.

The Essential Vampire Dentist's Apprentice Handbook   Volume 1

How to tame a tooth fairy

1. Find a tooth fairy
2. Tame it
3. Steal at least five teeth and give them to Viscount Bloodsucker

---

"Is this it?" I said, staring at the page. "There aren't many instructions!" No wonder Clot found Tooth Fairy Taming hard.

Fruity the bat clicked her tongue and whizzed ahead.

She'd spotted something.

"It's that way," said Clot, pointing after Fruity to a gold light glowing in the gloom. It looked very far away.

Still, at least the full moon lit our path.

We stomped.

And squelched.

And plodded.

And ... stopped.

A noise echoed through the droopy trees.

Wawhooool!

A howling noise.

Wawhooooooool!

A howling noise that was getting louder.

That's when I remembered where we had to go next.

PAST THE WEREWOLVES' DEN!

"Clot, this full moon," I said, looking at the sky. "It won't be a problem, will it? With the werewolves?"

Wawhooooooool!

Clot's eyes widened and her mouth formed an enormous 'O'.

"Shh!" she said.

"Shh" wasn't the answer I wanted.

Fruity landed on Clot's shoulder and shook.

"We should go back," whispered Clot. "The werewolves don't like dentists either." Her shoulders fell.

The first Unspeakable Circus performance was tomorrow night. And Norma and Twinkle were already trapped there. We had to get those tooth fairy teeth now.

"Is there another way to reach the marigolds?" I asked, looking between Clot and Fruity.

Clot shook her head. "Our only hope is that they don't hear us."

WAWHOOOOL!

"Well, cans we walk VERY far behind the Werewolves' Den?" said Walloping. "I has met a werewolf once before and their fur makes me…"

Walloping's eyes watered and his body shook.

"**Ah-ah-ah-chooooooooo!**" My best friend sneezed with such force, he slipped on some swamp moss, stumbling backwards into a tree.

THUNK.

The trunk creaked, its leaves shook and fell, and the bushes rustled.

WAHWHOOOOOOOOOL!

Yep, you guessed it.

The werewolves heard us.

Apprentice name: Clot
Project: Fang Finding
Night: two

Things have taken a turn for the gloomier.

The Small and the giant have only gone and run away from school. So muggins here has to follow them. For scientific purposes, and their own safety. Not because I want them to be my friends or anything. I don't need friends. I am a lone vampire. But if I don't get that giant to be quiet, I could be an eaten vampire, too. Werewolves have never liked me much.

Teeth examined: 0
Matches: 0
Seconds before werewolves find us: 0

Chapter thirteen

WawooLUNA!

The werewolves howled.

WAHWOOOOOOL!

"This way," said Clot, leading us through the sludgy undergrowth. "Stay low and for darkness' sake, stay quiet!"

Staying low was easy for me. But the swamp plants only came up to Walloping's knees. How would we hide the rest of him?

"It's time for your best sneaking!" I told him.

Walloping nodded and tiptoed away from the howls.

CRUNCH.

SQUELCH.

CRACK!

"OUCH!"

"SHH!"

BANG!

"Careful, Walloping!"

"SHHHHH!"

"AH-AH-AH-CHOO!"

It was no good. We couldn't be quiet. Besides, I was sure the werewolves had taken this path. We stepped out into a clearing that looked like my whole class of giants had danced on it. Half the trees were upturned, with long sprawling roots. The other plants were flattened.

I gulped. Werewolves were strong!

The howls were louder now. They sounded different somehow.

WawooLUNA!

WawooLUNA!

WawooLUNA?

"Get back!" said Clot, pulling me behind the one tree that was still standing.

I wasn't fast enough.

A hairy creature with wild, red eyes, sharp, shiny

102

claws and a body twice my size sprang in front of me.

A werewolf.

It reared on its hindlegs and bared its teeth in a snarl.

Walloping sneezed.

"Oh dear," said Clot (in what I thought was a bit of an understatement). "He's got a cavity in his upper-left tooth. That really needs seeing to."

Would that stop a werewolf eating us?

"**WawoooLUNA?**" howled the werewolf, flaring its nostrils and giving us a great big sniff. Its snout was almost as big as Walloping's now very runny nose.

"Gets away from him!" said Walloping, tugging me backwards and shaking a giant fist at the werewolf.

Fruity squeaked and flapped high into the sky, flitting in panicked circles.

"**WawoooLUNA?**" howled the werewolf again. It thrashed its tail and looked wildly between us.

"Wait ... I think it's asking a question," I said, trying to work it out.

"Luna?" I repeated.

This time, the wolf howled and lowered his head. Six more wolves emerged from the darkness. They stood in a circle in the middle of the clearing.

"Oh great," said Clot, sploshing backwards into a swamp puddle. "You've called more of them!"

"**LUUUUNA!**" the wolves howled as one, tilting their snouts towards the moon.

Their faces reminded me of someone.

"Ahchoo! They looks just like Madame Bogbrush when Norma goes missing!" said Walloping, rubbing his eyes.

"Walloping, that's it!" I cried.

I stepped slowly towards the closest werewolf. "Is Luna one of your pack?" I asked.

More howling and paw padding.

"Be carefuls!' said Walloping, still pulling me back.

"Did the Unspeakable Circus steal her?" I asked.

Even louder howls.

"Stop it!" hissed Clot. "Hasn't anyone ever told you getting werewolves upset is a BAD idea?"

Fruity clicked in agreement.

The wolves snarled.

And growled.

And moved closer.

But I thought giants and vampires were scary – until I got to know them. Maybe werewolves weren't any different.

I held my hands up and used my best, calming voice. "The Unspeakable Circus stole our friends, too."

The werewolves whined and pawed at the ground.

I knew it. They were trying to find their friend. Just like us.

"We'll help you get Luna out," I said.

The wolves gave us another big sniff ... like they were smelling for fibs.

I kept my breathing steady and my hands up. Eventually …

… sniff …

… after sniff …

… after sniff …

The wolves lowered their heads and let us pass.

Phew.

I squashed the worry that if I couldn't stop the circus, I'd let Mum, Dad, the giants *and* the werewolves down.

Clot looked at the sky and shivered.

The moon had travelled halfway across it since we left school. "If we're going to find that tooth before sunrise, we've got to move," she said.

The glowing white lights that were so far away when we set off were getting closer.

It was time to meet the tooth fairies.

Chapter fourteen

Sweet Dreams

Walloping skipped towards the glowing marsh marigolds. "Oooh, they is so pretty!" he said.

"Careful!" I cried. "Don't stomp on any fairies!"

Walloping stopped – his left boot hovered in mid-air over a shaking white flower. He stepped back just in time.

The air filled with sweet, soft music.

Your tooth, your tooth, we'll tell you the truth.

We'll give you lots of silver if you give us your tooth!

Dancing, golden lights emerged from the flower petals.

I swayed in time to the tune, my head lolling from side to side.

It was hypnotic.

"Don't look at them!" snapped Clot, covering her eyes. "Just find the tooth and go!"

Why wouldn't I look at them? The fairies were beautiful.

"Their little wings is so sweet" giggled Walloping.

"SWEET?" said the fairies. "YES, EAT SWEETS! EAT LOTS OF DELICIOUS SWEETS, THEN YOUR TEETH WILL FALL OUT AND WE CAN STEAL THEM ALL!"

The fairies danced faster and faster.

"SWEETS! SWEETS! SWEETS! TEETH! TEETH! TEETH!" they chanted.

My stomach ached at the thought of sweets.

"Don't even think about eating their sweets!" said Clot. Her eyes were still covered. Fruity had a wing over her eyes, too.

"OH, IGNORE THE VAMPIRE. SHE'S SUCH A SPOIL

SPORT!" said the closest fairy. "YOU'RE HUNGRY.
FOLLOW US TO OUR HUGE PALACE OF SWEETS!"

"YES! THE PALACE!" said the fairies. "IT TOOK YEARS
TO BUILD SUCH A VAST, GREAT AND HUMUNGOUS
TOWER, YOU MUST SEE IT!" They danced ahead in a
wobbly golden line.

I followed.

"Get back here!" said Clot, tugging my shoulder.
"You don't have time to taste sweets! We've got to be
home by dawn, remember?"

Surely one sweet wouldn't hurt!

The tiredness of another long night of failing
to save my friends hit me like a giant's stomping
boot.

Sweets would wake me up.

We followed the fairies in a daze.

Round in circles.

Through the swamp.

Towards the sweet, sweet smell of sweets.

Then, I saw it.

Right there in the middle of the swamp, surrounded
by marsh marigolds.

A gleaming white sweetshop made ENTIRELY OF
TEETH!

Some of the teeth were perfectly clean. Others were old and yellowing and sugar-coated.

"Is this it?" said Walloping with a frown. The fairies' "vast tower" barely reached the top of my best friend's head.

"**COME IN**," said the fairies, flitting inside. "**TRY SOME ROCK-HARD STICKS OF ROCK. OR MAYBE SOME EXTRA-STICKY CARAMEL!**"

My mouth watered.

Clot retched. "Can't you see what they're doing?" she moaned. "The fairies want to rot your teeth so they can steal them! They're the reason the swamp stinks of bad breath and tooth decay!"

"**SHUT IT**," said the Queen of the Tooth Fairies (she had a tiny crown and wore a sweatshirt with "Queen" embroidered

across it). She waved what could have been a wand, or a lollipop, or both, at Clot. "YOUR TEETH-STEALING KIND AREN'T WELCOME HERE. I DON'T INVITE YOU IN, VAMPIRE!"

Whoosh!

Crash!

The queen's words sent Clot flying backwards through the air, landing her bum-first in a bush.

So that's why Clot failed her Tooth Fairy Taming class.

It was up to Walloping and me now.

I stepped inside the toothy sweetshop and breathed in the delicious, sugary smells. There were jars of sweets, packets of sweets, shelves of sweets – all in the brightest colours and wrappers.

Walloping wrinkled his nose before squeezing inside the shop. His head hit the ceiling. "Does you have any bogweed sandwiches?" he asked the fairies. "Or maybe a three-headed worm? Mmm!"

As he spoke, his elbow sent a jar of rainbow jellybeans rolling over the floor.

"Oops!" he cried, bending to pick them up and swiping a shelf of gummy animals and fudge boxes, which also went flying.

If Walloping knocked the whole place down, collecting loose teeth would be easy. But I doubted the fairies built shops with their rarest teeth.

"DON'T MOVE, WE'LL BRING THE SWEETS TO YOU!" said the fairies, trying their best to tidy the tumbling lemon drops and liquorice sticks.

They flapped towards me, holding a swirly red and yellow lollipop on a tiny velvet cushion. The smell of rhubarb and custard hit me instantly. They gave Walloping a toffee with "Tooth Ripper" marked on the wrapper.

"Why is dis do d-d-sticky?" Walloping struggled to say through his toffee-stuck teeth.

My lollipop tasted good.

Sooooo good.

I smiled dreamily.

I could curl up right here and snooze.

"THAT'S RIGHT, REST!" said the fairies.

Walloping swayed from side to side.

I leaned against my friend, and all my worries faded away.

I closed my eyes.

Observations:

Oh sweet success! The vampires are so busy dying their hair, they haven't even noticed that WE have their patients. And we're filling them with sweets!

We predict this year's vampire school photo will be yet another flop. Doubt it will convince a single creature to pay them a visit. But we should still take the usual precautions.

Recommendations:

Keep whispering in the ears of sleeping swamp creatures, reminding them to stay away from the dentist.

And keep the Small and the giant here until after the photo.

Chapter fifteen

Don't Let the Tooth Fairies Bite

I was in the middle of the sweetest dream, when a cry from Clot of "*Find the tooth and get out!*" cut through my snooze. And just in time.

A fairy was clamped on my cheek, bashing my front tooth with a tiny hammer.

"Oi!" I said, batting her away.

"OH, SORRY!" said the fairy. "WERE YOU USING THAT TOOTH? IT LOOKED A BIT WOBBLY!"

At that moment, Walloping woke, too. "Ahh! Gerroff me!" he cried, flapping at three chisel-waving tooth fairies circling his mouth. "Let's go, Best Friend! I has done enough exploring of the tooth fairies!"

We couldn't go yet. Not if the tooth that chained our friends to the circus was here.

Outside, I spotted Clot gesturing wildly. She pointed *behind* the palace of sweets.

I knew what to do.

"Can I have another lollipop, please?" I asked the fairies. "To eat outside. I enjoy lollipops even more in the stinking swamp air!" I fibbed. The fairies flapped, cheered and filled my hands with boiled sweets, gummy animals and lollipops.

My stomach groaned. I wished I could eat the lot.

I squeezed past Walloping.

"Stay there, I'll be right back!" I said, as casually as possible.

I'd be sneakier on my own.

Unfortunately, Walloping didn't know what I was planning.

"Wait for me!" he said.

There was a *bang* and *crash* and whiff of sherbet powder as Walloping poked his head out the tiny sweetshop door. "Oh no, oh no, oh no! I is stuck!" he cried! "Help!"

I *should* help my best friend right away.

But …

… he was being a brilliant distraction!

"GIANT NUMBSKULL, STOP BREAKING OUR DOOR!" cursed the fairies. "YOU CAN'T LEAVE. YOU HAVEN'T HAD A CHOCOLATE SWAMP GOBLIN YET!"

I shot Walloping an apologetic look before dashing round the back of the shop.

Clot was right! There were rows of sweet jars, as big as barrels. They had labels like *Cute Baby Teeth*. *Stinky Grown-Up Teeth*. And *Manky Molars*. At the end of the row was one jar, much smaller than the rest, marked *Super-Rare Fangs and Gnashers*. There was a single gleaming fang inside it.

Super-Rare Fangs and Gnashers? My brain fizzed and it had nothing to do with the popping candy in my lollipop.

Viscount Bloodsucker said the creature that bit the Never-Ending Contract and chained my friends to the circus was rare. I pulled the fang from the jar and poked it inside the bite marks on Norma's contract.

My heart leapt. It was the *perfect* fit! Now all we needed was Clot to tell us what creature it belonged to. I pushed the tooth into my pocket.

Then, remembering Clot's Tooth Fairy Taming test, I pocketed five manky molars from the next jar along, too.

"Heeeeelp!" moaned Walloping.

I ran back to my best friend. The teeth clinked together in my pockets and stuck out at odd angles. I hoped the fairies wouldn't notice.

"Why did you leaves me?" said Walloping. His eyes filled with tears.

I squirmed.

I'd let him down.

Again.

While I'd been gone, the fairies had tied liquorice shoelaces round Walloping's middle to heave him out the door.

I pulled my best everything-is-normal-and-I-don't-have-pockets-stuffed-full-of-stolen-teeth face.

"Hold on, I'll get you out," I said, grabbing a couple of laces and tugging as hard as I could.

Until …

With a *pull* …

… a *pop* …

… and a tinkle of falling teeth …

Walloping shot from the shop door and crashed beside Clot in the bushes.

"Let's go!" I cried as Walloping staggered to his feet.

I was too slow.

The Tooth Fairy Queen pointed at my bulging pockets and shrieked: "**THE SMALL'S STOLEN OUR TEETH! BITE HIM!**"

Gnash, gnash, gnash.

And hundreds of angry tooth fairies headed straight for me.

Apprentice name: Clot
Project: Fang Finding
Night: two, continued

Running and reporting is hard!
What did I tell them? Don't. Eat. The. Sweets.
What did they do?
Eat the sweets.
No one listens to Clot.
But, I think the Small has a tooth match.
Hard to tell between all the "owwing" and running!
Must sit down.
Can't sit down.
Can't lose tooth.
If I keep running, maybe I'll pass the project.
Maybe I'll join the other dentists in class.
Maybe I won't be so alone.
Maybe.
If we ever make it back to Happy Fang ...

Teeth examined: I
Matches: I?
Hours until sunrise: I

Chapter sixteen

A New Day Dawns

"Owwww!" I wailed. A tooth fairy bite might be small, but it hurts like salt in a paper cut.

"You gets away from him!" said Walloping. He waggled his fists at the fairies, while Fruity squawked and Clot … well, Clot kept looking at the sky and telling us to "hurry up". I thought she'd be pleased we'd stolen teeth for her and almost finished the project. She looked even grumpier than usual.

I wanted to hurry too. Now we'd found the fang, Clot said we had to get back to school to figure out which creature it came from.

But boy was I sleepy. My vision swam in and out of focus. The fairy bite made me woozy. Walloping looked tired too. He stretched his arms high, shaking leaves off the trees as we stumbled on.

Clot flapped her arms in front of us. "Seriously, will you two speed up? The night's nearly over!"

Walloping's stomach growled.

"I'll go super speedily, just as soon as I've had this sandwich!" said Walloping, suddenly stomping ahead.

"Sandwich?" I asked. "What sandwich?"

SNAP!

"Aaaaahhh!" cried Walloping.

My best friend hovered horizontally in mid-air, kicking his legs like he was in a swimming pool!

"Oh, for cavity's sake!" said Clot.

"Squawk," said Fruity.

A pair of slimy, leafy jaws clamped around my best friend. And I couldn't see any sandwiches.

"A Deadly Creature-Eating Plant?" said Clot. "Didn't I tell you we were in a hurry, WHAT are you doing in there?!"

The plant made worrying munching sounds.

Nom, nom, nom.

"I was so hungry! All I has eaten in ages was that horrible tooth-ripper toffee from those pesky tooth fairies," said Walloping, holding his jaw. "Then, we walks past a giant swampfish and bogweed sandwich, just floating in fronts of us. I knows it might be someone's dinner,

but I only takes a tiny bite!" Walloping sniffed. "But the nasty sandwich bites me back!"

Nom, nom, nom, went the plant.

"That's how the Creature-Eater catches its dinner!" said Clot. "It disguises itself as your favourite foods!"

Nom, nom, nom, went the plant, munching on Walloping's right boot.

Clot looked at the sky. It had a hint of pink.

I shook the plant's stem. I tapped its leaves. And I grabbed Walloping's arms, struggling to pull him free.

Nothing worked.

"Out the way," said Clot, pushing me aside and pulling out a pair of rubber gloves and a toothbrush from inside her cloak. "Okay, Plant," she said, waving her toothbrush at it. "Drop the giant or I'm cleaning your teeth."

Nom, nom … aww!

THUD!

The Creature-Eating Plant plonked Walloping on the ground.

Even plants with excellent teeth were scared of having them cleaned!

"Thanks for getting me out," said Walloping, wiping plant drool off his bottom.

"Yeah, well. Couldn't let our guests get eaten," Clot muttered.

Luckily, Walloping was still in one piece … well, except for one gobbled stomping boot.

CHIRPY, CHIRPY, TWEET!

Swamp birds circled overhead.

"The Swamp Flappers aren't supposed to be out at night," said Walloping.

Clot moaned, covering her head in her hands. "I told you to hurry. Now we're too late. The dawn's coming!"

The sky was lighter.

"Don't be silly!" said Walloping, hopping along on his one good boot. "We can still make it back before the sun burns you!"

Fruity clicked her tongue and tugged on Clot's shoulder.

"Of course we can make it," I said. "The mountain's just over there." (It looked miles away, but I wasn't going to say that.)

Clot shook her head. "I've only been undead for 700 years. I'm too young to really die."

Clot couldn't give up. "Walloping can carry us!" I tried. "If we hop fast, I bet we'll beat sunrise."

"Good idea!" said Walloping, scooping Clot and me up. Fruity flapped above us.

And we were off.

Walloping hopped.

And squelched.

And splashed.

And stopped for breath.

And hopped again, even faster this time. He pounded through the sludge, leapt sink pits and ignored heckles from the Moaning Marsh.

"That's it! Keep going!" I cried.

I tried not to think about the sky getting lighter … and lighter … and lighter.

We were so close to the bottom of the mountain!

"Stop," said Clot.

"Huh?" said Walloping, stumbling to a halt.

"Stories say how beautiful the sunrise is," she said. "If I'm not going to make it, I'd like to watch it."

Clot stroked Fruity's wings and whispered, "Be free, Fruity. No use being stuck with me."

Fruity didn't move. She just blinked and squawked.

"I said 'go!'" said Clot, shaking the little bat off her arm.

Fruity squawked and stayed put.

Clot shook her some more. "Please, I don't want you to see this!"

Fruity hesitated, hovering above Clot's head before giving one last squawk and flapping up the mountain.

"Clot this is ridiculous, you can't give up!" I said. "Walloping, keep going!"

Walloping hopped off again.

"I said 'STOP!'" said Clot.

Walloping wobbled to another one-legged stop. His face filled with worry and confusion.

A golden glow of sunlight crept through the droopy trees, hitting our faces.

We were too late.

Chapter seventeen

Burn

The sky was pink.

The birds were cheeping.

And the sun bounced off the swamp, filling it with light.

Clot and me were still sitting on Walloping's shoulders. I flapped my arms in front of Clot, trying to stop the sun catching her.

"No," said Clot, pushing me away. "Let me see the dawn." She took a deep breath and looked straight ahead. "It's beautiful," she gasped.

"Clot, please!" I said, leaning my whole body over to shade her. She pushed me back again. That's when I really started to panic.

How would she burn?

Would she crumble to ash in a flash?

Would flames start at her toes and lick and flick up her cloak?

Clot held her hands to her heart and whispered, "Goodbye, lonely world!"

Walloping sniffed, letting a giant tear splash onto the ground.

We waited.

Clot took a deep breath.

We waited.

I wriggled anxiously on Walloping's shoulder. The spikey, raspberry-blowing, can-can-dancing, cymbal-crashing worry creature in the pit of my stomach taunted me. What kind of Chosen One lets someone *burn*?

We waited.

I couldn't wait any more.

We waited.

This was unbearable.

"Clot?" said Walloping, eventually. "Since you isn't dead ... or at least you is no more dead than you already was ... can we go back to school now? I is tired and hungry!"

Clot blinked in the sun. "I don't understand," she said. She held her arms out in front of her, moving one, then the other. It was like she couldn't believe they were still there.

"Viscount Bloodsucker always said that ..."

WHOOSH!

Well, that was freaky! Clot mentioned the Headteacher's name and one second later Viscount Bloodsucker, surrounded by a cloud of flapping fruit bats, appeared in front of us.

Fruity was at the front of the pack. She hadn't abandoned Clot! She wrapped her wings around Clot's arm, leaving the other bats circling overhead like one big, bat-shaped sun umbrella.

Viscount Bloodsucker covered his face with his cloak. "Dracula's Doo Dahs! Clot, what are you doing? You know vampires burn in the sun!"

I half-expected Viscount Bloodsucker to burst into flame. I *didn't* expect him to hand Clot a tube of SUNTAN LOTION. The extra gloopy factor 50 stuff Mum makes me wear at the seaside!

"Viscount Bloodsucker, are you saying vampires are scared of *sunburn*?" I asked, hardly believing it.

Everything I thought I knew about vampires was wrong.

They weren't scary.

They didn't go around biting people.

And they got sunburn like the rest of us!

The Headteacher shook his fists at the sky. "We despise sunburn! White fangs and red faces do NOT look good together. Sun cream keeps us looking youthfully dead and fresh!" He ran a hand through his perfect black hair. "Being outside like this the day before our big photo shoot is completely irresponsible!"

Clot looked up at the Viscount and did something I'd never seen her do before.

She giggled.

And laughed.

And smiled a smile so big it would have filled Walloping's face!

It was a smile that made me want to smile, too!

"I'm still here! I didn't burn!" Clot sprang from Walloping's shoulder and twirled through the swamp, tossing her head back and laughing. She pulled me down from Walloping's shoulders and flung her arms round me in a humungous hug.

"And Clot collected five teeth to pass her Tooth Fairy Taming test," I said, handing the five manky molars to the Viscount. "I have the BEST news, too!" I added, reaching for the super-rare fang. "We've found the type of tooth that bit the Never-Ending Contract! So, you can tell us where it comes from."

"Enough!" snapped the Viscount, holding up his hand. "It is far too early to be identifying teeth. You must get a perfect day's sleep to look your welcoming best tomorrow."

Did the Headteacher sound *disappointed* I'd found the fang?

"Come," he said. He raised his arms and hissed.

The cloud of bats circled lower and squawked.

Before I knew what was happening, I was hovering above Walloping's shoulders.

Then I lifted higher, up past the dangling tree tops.

I'd learned lots of things since moving to the swamp. Flying wasn't one of them.

"Eek! What's going on?" cried Walloping. My best friend was drifting too – but his legs dangled a lot closer to the trees, which he kept crashing into.

"It's the bats!" said Clot, swooping and whooping above us. "They're carrying us home." She giggled

132

again,
before
bursting
into song.

"*Oh what a wonderful time,*

To be – well – not quite alive

Oh, I'm feeling oh so fine

I saw the sun, and I didn't die!"

"Come on, sing along!" she cried.

So, we did. There was Clot, my best friend and me, flapping through the dawn sky, singing.

For a minute or two, I almost forgot my friends were still in danger.

But down in the depths of the swamp, someone had spotted us.

Someone who wanted to cause unspeakable trouble.

Vampire Surveillance Report: #1239

Tooth Fairy: Bonnie Bonbon

Observations:

Gobstoppers! Those thieving swamp creatures are on the way back to Happy Fang with OUR rarest fang. They must be stopped. If their school photo is a success, it could put an end to our tooth supplies.

Recommendations:

I'll keep following the thieves, but I need backup. Call in the zombie clowns.

Chapter eighteen

The Unexpected Delivery

Giants are noisy sleepers. But as long as you stuff socks in your ears, you'll snooze through their snoring.

Waking up next to vampires wasn't so easy.

On the third night, I woke to the unmistakeable feeling of a toothpick being jammed up my nose.

"Oops, did I disturb you?" said Floss, wiping the pick on my bedsheet. "I wanted to see if Smalls had any teeth in their nostrils, you know, like the seven-snouted marsh mouse,"

"We don't," I said, wiggling my picked nose.

"And I wanted to tell you about the delivery!" Floss added, grinning.

"No, I saw it first!" said Gargle, rushing over so fast he almost tripped on his cloak.

"The delivery?" I said, sitting up.

"I said *I'm* giving it to him!" said Floss.

Floss and Gargle ducked down under the bed. They popped up again holding a large cardboard box.

It had the slightest green glow.

"It's a special delivery!" said Floss. I rubbed my eyes. For a moment, I thought she was glowing, too.

"We signed for it ourselves!" said Gargle. "But it's addressed to you, Harvey!" Gargle handed the box to me. He was grinning from ear to ear.

"I've got post?" I said. It wasn't my birthday. Even if it had been, Mum didn't know my address here. And why was it *glowing*?

Walloping was awake now, too. He rattled the box. "Aww," he said. "It doesn't sound like sandwiches!"

The handwriting on the front didn't look like Mum's. Or Dad's.

There was a stamp on the bottom that said *UC Supplies*.

"Ooooh! Looks like someone's been shopping

at Ultra Clean!" said Clot, twirling to my side. She grinned at me before bursting into song. "*Ultra Clean, Ultra Clean, Ultra Clean makes teeth gleam*!" She was like a different vampire now she'd survived the dawn. I'd never seen her so happy.

But I was confused.

I hadn't done any shopping.

I picked up the box.

My hands glowed green.

"Come on, open it!" said Clot, dancing from foot to foot.

"Yes, open it!" chanted the other apprentices, crowding around the bed.

I wanted to know what was inside, too.

I tore the box.

The first thing I saw was a letter.

Dear Harvey and Walloping,
Why haven't you come back to school yet?
Hurry up and get the answers we need
from Viscount Bloodsucker and break those
Never-Ending Circus Chains.
Harvey, you're our Chosen One. We're
counting on you.

Love and stomping,
Madame Bogbrush.
PS. Here are some gifts to charm the Viscount.
Those vampires are suckers for hair dye and
toothpaste.

Madame Bogbrush sent the parcel! There couldn't be anything to worry about if it came from the Headteacher.

Walloping poked around the box. He pulled out bottles of black hair dye and tubes of charcoal toothpaste. "Madame Bogbrush could have sent us some three-headed worms," he said, emptying the box.

"No way! This is the best present ever!" said Clot, Gargle and Floss, who each grabbed a tube of toothpaste.

I pulled out the rare fang I'd found last night. Now the apprentices were in a good mood, I bet they'd help us.

"Do any of you recognise this tooth?" I said, holding it up to the vampires.

Their eyes widened.

"Put that away!" said Clot. "This is MY project, remember?"

That didn't stop Gargle flipping through the pages of his *Advanced Tooth-Finding Manual*.

"I can't believe it!" he said, "I've never seen a ..."

Gargle was about to tell me what he'd never seen, when the dorm door flew open.

Swoosh!

Viscount Bloodsucker swept in front of us. His eyes twinkled and he clapped his hands.

"Happy Photo Night, apprentices!" he said with a bow. "The photographer is waiting for us. So ... oh my fangs, what's this?" said Viscount Bloodsucker, clocking the glowing green box. "Gifts? How marvellous!" he said, looking inside my unexpected delivery. "My favourite brand of hair dye! How did you know? And charcoal toothpaste, what a treat!"

The Viscount turned back to the apprentices. "One last tooth polish for luck, then it's time to strike a pose!"

He handed out the rest of the toothpaste tubes and squeezed a thick black dollop of paste on a brush for himself. Then he turned to me. "I must say, this is very kind of you. Perhaps it's even a sign us vampires are making good friends in the swamp at last!"

"Yes," I said, not wanting to disappoint him. He had to help us now.

"Viscount Bloodsucker," I began, still clutching the rare fang. "Here's the fang I found. The one that bit the contract." I held it up to him.

A look flashed across Viscount Bloodsucker's face, like he'd eaten a rotten swampfish. Then he waved his hand. "Later, later, we've got a photoshoot to prepare for," he said, swooshing away.

Walloping bent down and hissed in my ear. "That is the second time the Viscount doesn't help us when he promised he was going to."

I tried to stay positive. "I guess he's too worried about his photo to talk," I said. "Anyway, I think

Gargle found the fang in his book. Let's follow him to the bathrooms and ask."

We dashed after the apprentices.

In the bathroom, hundreds of shiny marble basins with gold taps lined the white tiled floor. I thought about the swamp sludge that oozed from the walls in the giants' bathrooms. I bet Walloping had never seen a place like this.

"It's horrible! Just horrible!" my best friend wailed. He watched the apprentices squeeze their charcoal toothpaste onto their brushes, shaking his head in disgust.

But when the brushing was done, Walloping scowled. He scooped me up, so my face was level with his. "Are you sure that special toothpaste you gives the vampires makes teeth white?" He pointed at the apprentices.

Vampires don't like mirrors.

So, they hadn't seen what Walloping had seen ... yet.

"*Aaaaaaaaaaahhhhhhh!*"

Okay, now they'd seen it.

I wanted to scream, too.

Chapter nineteen

Blackout

"Oh Harvey," said Walloping, "What has we done?" The apprentices dashed into The Cavity, yelling for Viscount Bloodsucker. "They're black! Our teeth are black!" they cried, throwing the toothpaste tubes at his feet and pointing at their fangs in horror.

Viscount Bloodsucker paled. His fangs were black, too.

The photographer, a quivering bogeygirl with an old-fashioned camera slung round her neck, shook her raggedy head. "What fresh horror is this?" she said. Her eyes glistened like two muddy puddles. "I knew I shouldn't have come!" She turned and half-ran, half-drifted down the mountain, leaving only a cloud of dust behind her.

"Wait! Don't go!" said Viscount Bloodsucker, chasing after her. "You promised this year's photo would be the best ever!"

"I don't understand," I said. "Charcoal toothpaste washes straight out!"

I picked up a toothpaste tube and gave it a sniff.

Uh oh.

"I don't think this is toothpaste," I whispered to Walloping. "It's … hair dye." The vampires had dyed their teeth!

"WHAT did you do?" said the Headteacher, stalking back up the mountain without the photographer. He pointed a long, shaky finger at me.

"There must be a mistake!" I said. Madame Bogbrush wouldn't get us in trouble.

"Ultra Clean supplies never makes mistakes!" he said.

Hmm. There was something strange about that box from the start.

Normal boxes don't glow.

"The toothpaste wasn't from Ultra Clean Supplies!" I said. The truth smacked me like the gnashers of a Deadly Creature-Eating Plant. "It's from the Unspeakable Circus!" I cried. "It's a trick!"

Walloping slapped his hand over his mouth.

The vampire apprentices hushed.

"But … you're supposed to be our friends," said Floss. Her voice trembled.

"You promised you'd make our photo even better!" said Gargle.

"Why did you let the Unspeakable Circus *dye* our teeth?" said Floss and Gargle together. "You'll make the swamp creatures even more afraid of us!"

"That's not true!" said Walloping. "Giants doesn't mind brown teeth!"

The bats flapped angrily around us, shooting poo pellets all over the place (including on my head).

The apprentices turned their backs. Apart from Clot. Clot twirled between the gravestones, singing a new song.

"*Charcoal teeth! Charcoal teeth!*

Charcoal teeth make the swamp go EEK!"

"It's not our fault!" I said. "We didn't give you that toothpaste, the Unspeakable Circus did!" As I said it, another worry hit me. Gargle and Floss said they signed for the delivery.

144

I pulled back the edge of Gargle's cloak. His wrist glowed green underneath it. Floss pulled her own cloak back. There was a glowing green chain around her, too.

"What's happening?" cried Floss, shaking her arm.

The green chains of light twisted and tightened.

"Make it stop!" said Gargle.

But Walloping and I already knew: we couldn't make it stop.

The apprentices clung to their friends. It was no good.

The light pulled Gargle and Floss down the mountain. They belonged to the circus now.

"No. Not again. She can't steal from me again," said Viscount Bloodsucker. He collapsed against a gravestone, head in hands.

"Oh dear, oh dear, oh dear. This be bad news!" said Walloping.

"Viscount Bloodsucker!" I said, running up to the Headteacher. "You HAVE to tell us what bit the contracts. It's our only way to save Gargle, Floss and every other creature the circus has stolen!"

I waved the rare fang at him once more. Surely he'd help us now.

"I … can't!" he wailed. Big tears plopped around his feet. "Just go. You've caused enough trouble by coming here," he murmured.

"Viscount, please!" I said, shaking his shoulder. He clearly knew what creature that tooth belonged to. Why wouldn't he tell us?

"*LEAVE*. I don't invite you in. You're not welcome here. Ever!"

The other apprentices scrubbed at their teeth and moaned.

"Someone must recognise this fang?" I said, waving it in front of as many apprentices as possible.

"Hmph," said the vampires, one by one. They tilted their heads away from us. None of them would even LOOK at the tooth.

None of them apart from … Clot. She skipped towards me and whispered in my ear. "It's time for the truth," she said. "I've checked the textbooks. I know what bit your contract!"

How to identify swamp creature teeth

First, look at the tooth
1. Is it (A) pointy or (B) nobbly?
2. Is it so sharp it draws blood? (A) No (B) Ouch
3. What does it smell like? (A) Perfection (B) Oranges (C) Mouldy cheese (D) Despair
4. What colour is it? (A) Sludge brown (B) Candlelit yellow (C) Raincloud grey (D) Algae green (E) Bat black (F) Fresh snow white.

For answers, turn to pages 167–203

Chapter twenty

The Truth

Clot pulled Walloping and me down the craggy slope of the mountain until we were out of earshot of the wailing vampires.

At last, we were going to get answers. We'd break the circus chains and save Floss, Gargle, Luna the werewolf, Norma Enormous and Twinkle. *And* stop zombie lions eating my classmates. I wasn't going to disappoint everyone. I'd be a proper Chosen One!

"Well? What bites the contracts?" said Walloping, hopping from foot to foot, sending rocks sliding down the slope.

I held the tooth out to Clot, struggling to keep my hand steady.

"Hey, it looks just like one of *your* teeth!" said Walloping, waggling his finger at Clot's mouth.

To my surprise, she blushed and pulled her hand over her mouth. "It's not mine," she mumbled through her hand. "It's … a grown-up vampire fang! You can tell because it's so shiny and perfect. I wonder how those rotten tooth fairies got their wings on it!" She paused and looked at the rocky ground. "I didn't want to tell you at first, because if you found out, you'd tell the other swamp creatures. Then they'd *never* visit us. And you'd never be friends with me."

I gaped at Clot. I didn't even realise she wanted to be our friend!

But also … I was right all along: a vampire *did* bite the contracts. And I knew who was to blame.

"Viscount Bloodsucker did this!" I cried.

Clot shook her head. "It can't be him," she said. Although the wobble in her voice made her sound less sure.

"A good vampire dentist would never break the no-biting rule," she said. "Except …"

"Except what?" said Walloping and me together.

"I bit a pair of my favourite socks once, to stop them getting holes in," she said. "I wanted them to last forever. And, well, one little vampire bite can do that. Now my socks will never die!" She lifted her cloak to reveal a pair of glowing green socks with black and orange stripes. The stripes were the same colours as Fruity. The little bat was dozing on her wrist again.

Somewhere up the mountain, I heard shouts and footsteps.

"CLO-O-O-T! GET BACK HERE!" Viscount Bloodsucker's voice boomed through the mountains. He'd stopped sobbing long enough to spot she'd gone. "YOU'LL BE POLISHING TEETH BY YOURSELF FOR A YEAR FOR THIS!" he roared.

"We need to get further into the swamp," I said, running through the sludge. "Clot, can anything undo a vampire bite?" I asked, ducking under low-hanging swamp trees and jumping puddles.

So far, we knew none of these things worked:

- Burning with torches
- Burning in the sun
- Ripping
- Stomping
- Tearing
- Shredding

Clot scratched her chin. "Ooh, I don't think we've ever tried to reverse undeath," she said.

Reverse undeath.

"Reverse! That's it!" I said, almost slipping on the swamp weeds.

"Is it?" said Walloping, scratching his head.

I felt inside my pocket and pulled out the silver dentist's mirror I'd pocketed on our first night.

"Careful where you're waving that!" said Clot, leaping away from me. "I haven't got time to stare at myself now."

"Viscount Bloodsucker said mirrors reverse your image. What if mirrors reverse other things too?" I said.

"You means, like the contract and circus chains?" said Walloping, catching on.

"Exactly!" I pulled out the contract again and lay it as smoothly as I could on a knobbly rock.

Clot winced and covered her eyes.

Walloping leaned over the page.

I waved the tiny mirror over the paper and …

… the bottom left corner let off the smallest green spark. The chain of light weaving out of it and towards Norma (wherever she was) was as strong as ever.

"Is that it?" said Walloping. He picked up the paper and shook it. "That won't save Norma Enormous!"

"We're going to need a bigger mirror," I said.

"Like the Narcissus?" said Clot, clapping her hands.

"The what?" said Walloping and me.

"Our lost mirror. The one that hung in reception. It was huge! They say Viscount Bloodsucker's never been quite the same since it was stolen."

"And ... do you know who took it?" I asked. My heart beat a little faster.

"Of course," she said. "The Unspeakable Circus. But they move so much, we never know where they are. Every time we think we've caught them they disappear into the night."

So that's why Viscount Bloodsucker looked cross every time I mentioned the circus. It didn't explain why a vampire bit the contracts in the first place, though. I still thought the Headteacher was up to something. But right now, we had some contract reversing to do.

I looked down at Norma's contract. It glowed as brightly as ever. "I know how to find the circus," I said.

"How?" said Clot and Walloping together.

"We follow the light."

Vampire Surveillance Report: #1240

Tooth Fairy: Bonnie Bonbon

Observations:

Our Unspeakable friends came to the rescue with that tooth-dyeing trick! The giant and the Small have left Happy Fang for good. The photo was a disaster. No one will be visiting the dentist for at least another year. Phew!

Recommendations:

Send double portions of toffee eclairs and gummy zombie clowns to the Unspeakable Circus's sweetshop.

And make sure the Small and giant never steal another tooth again ...

Chapter twenty-one

The Poster

Walloping wasn't happy with me.

"I still doesn't think we should go anywhere near the Unspeakable Circus before we is sure we can breaks Norma's, Twinkle's, Luna's, Gargle's and Floss's Never-Ending Contracts," he said. He'd stomped through the swamp extra loudly since I'd told him my plan.

STOMP.

CLOMP.

SPLASH.

SNAP.

Clot, on the other hand, was singing again.

"*Oh what a beautiful night.*

Following this little green light.
Things will be more than alright.
Now I have seen the daylight.
Doobedobedoobedoo, Ah!"

Fruity the bat flapped above her head and squawked.

"Shh!" I whispered to them. "We don't want the Ring Mistress to hear us!"

I knew we were going the right way. The green glow from the circus was getting brighter by the second. Soon a circus tent taller than three Wallopings loomed ahead of us. Around it were three smaller tents and rows of wonky caravans. And ... was that a queue? A wobbly line of tiny creatures with cat-like ears and flapping wings scuttled around outside the Big Top. The Ring Mistress didn't just have a circus now, she had an audience.

"Ooh, what's that?" said Clot. She pointed at a poster nailed on a nearby swamp tree.

"Is that ... you?" she asked.

My stomach twisted more than a bowl of spaghetti. Clot was right. There was a picture of ME right in the middle of the poster. The Ring Mistress knew I was coming.

Walloping blocked my path. "I says it was a bad idea coming here! I is not letting my best friend get eatens!"

I didn't want to get eaten either. But what would Mum and Dad say if they heard I'd run away? No one would be proud of me then.

Somewhere nearby I heard the clank of chains and a sad "*Rurooghaaaa.*"

I'd recognise the sound of our skelephant friend anywhere. "It's Twinkle!" I cried, pointing to the tallest tree behind the Big Top and running under Walloping's legs. "Quick! The Ring Mistress has chained her up again."

Twinkle raised her trunk when she saw us, but all her usual twinkle had gone out. "Oh, Twinkle!" I said, hugging as much of her as I could reach.

She stomped her foot, but she couldn't free it from the clanking metal chain or the one made of glowing green light.

That decided it.

We weren't running away. Even though the rattling, wailing sounds coming from the circus caravans set my teeth on edge and the zombie lions wanted to eat me. "We'll get you out, I promise," I said.

"I doesn't like it here," said Walloping, peering over his shoulder at a sobbing bogeygirl hunched against another tree.

Twinkle wasn't the only performer the Ring Mistress had chained up.

There were wailing bogeyboys and girls, flailing fauns and other raggedly dressed children who could have been Smalls, chained to the trees. And Gargle and Floss, chained either side of the same tree, far from the others. "Please, open wider!" they called at the children closest to them. "We only want a quick look at your teeth! We've never been so close to so many swamp creatures!"

Could Gargle and Floss be *enjoying* themselves?

The other chained children cried and shook. I bet they'd been tricked into signing Never-Ending Contracts.

At the next tree, a girl with the wildest, knottiest hair I'd ever seen, hung her head and howled. When she spotted us, she made a noise that sounded like a growl, before saying, "I told you, I'm NOT wearing a pink leotard and I am NOT going on stage!"

She glared and snarled, crouching low like she was going to spring on us.

I knew who she must be.

"Are you … Luna? The werewolf?" I asked.

"You know I am," she growled.

"We isn't from the circus, we is here to rescue you, silly!" said Walloping in the world's loudest whisper.

The other children stopped crying and stared at us.

"It's true!" said Clot, popping out from behind Walloping's left knee. "Don't be sad! A new day will dawn soon, and it'll be marvellous, just marvellous!" She was still happy, even here.

"Ahhhh! Another dentist!" yelped Luna. "Get it away from me!"

Clot's shoulders sagged. I hoped one day the swamp creatures wouldn't be so scared of her.

"We promised your pack we'd get you out," I said. "But first, we need your Never-Ending Contract. And we need a giant mirror. We think there's one here, somewhere. Have you seen it?"

Luna howled again. "I don't know! All I know is if I keep refusing to go on stage, the Ring Mistress will leave me here to rot until I'm undead. Then I'll never escape!"

Luna's howling, Walloping's stomping and Clot's singing weren't helping us keep a low profile. Luckily, rehearsals were in full swing. Screechy, squeaky sounds of out-of-tune violins and dodgy trumpets rose from the Unspeakable Big Top.

159

Maybe, just maybe, the Ring Mistress wouldn't know we were here.

"Look! Look!" said Walloping, pointing at the biggest green and gold caravan behind the Big Top. It stood in front of a higgledy-piggledy row of foul-smelling food stalls promising *the tastiest rotten egg pies around.* And *buy one stick of mouldy floss, get one free!* And a tiny sweetshop made entirely of teeth offering *free sacks of gummy zombie clowns.* I gulped. It was no surprise the tooth fairies had a sweetshop here.

There was a huge sign in front of the caravan. It said:

TOP-SECRET STASH OF NEVER-ENDING CONTRACTS HERE. ABSOLUTELY NO ENTRY – ESPECIALLY FOR SMALLS AND GIANTS!

Hmm. A sign like that seemed a little too convenient to me. But before I could stop him, Walloping charged straight for the caravan.

"Walloping! Wait!" I dashed after him.

"It isn't even locked! Oh boy, we is so lucky!" said Walloping. He pushed the door open and squeezed himself inside. The caravan creaked and wobbled.

I peered around for signs of the Ring Mistress. Or a stray zombie lion. Or even a tooth fairy.

Clot bit her lip.

"You're worried about going in there, too?" I asked.

"No … I just can't go in," she said. "I'm not invited."

Before I could say that might be a good idea and she should stay out here and check for signs of trouble, Walloping said, "Come in, Clot!"

Great. Now both of them were inside the suspicious caravan.

"*Ruroogha!*" trumpeted Twinkle, rattling her chains behind us.

Walloping's arm poked out of an open window as he rummaged around inside. "It's okay, the contracts is here. I sees a big wooden chest that says 'Contracts' on it!"

Wow, we really were lucky!

I told myself off for being such a worrier and edged into the caravan. (With Walloping and Clot already inside, there wasn't much room.)

And there it was: Mistress Ring's old wooden trunk. The same one she hid her vanishing potions in last term.

I heaved the lid open and …

CLUNK.

THUNK.

CLINK!

The sides of the caravan fell away.

We weren't in a caravan.

We were in a cage!

Chapter twenty-two

Open Wide!

Okay, so I know what you're thinking.

What kind of Chosen One lets their friends go charging into a cage in the middle of the world's creepiest circus? And what kind of nincompoop follows them in?

Turns out, it's this nincompoop.

We were well and truly trapped.

I had no idea what we were going to do.

And, almost as terrifyingly, Walloping was jiggling around like he needed a wee.

"What's going on?" said Walloping, shaking the cage's iron bars.

Right on cue, the Ring Mistress appeared outside the cage to answer. Her green eyes flashed and her gold, lion-topped cane was shinier than ever. "How unspeakably wonderful of my newest performers to arrive so promptly," she said, smiling far too sweetly. "The zombie lions have been expecting you."

I remembered the circus poster and shuddered.

"You'll want these, I imagine," she said, pushing three new Never-Ending Contracts with our names on through the bars. Seeing my eyes widen, she added, "That's right, one for each of you."

"We'll never sign them, never!" I said, doing my best to sound brave. Although Walloping was now bobbing around so much, crossing and uncrossing his legs, I worried he might sign anything to get out of here.

The Ring Mistress snorted. "Mine is the greatest, finest, most unspeakably unspeakable circus to ever exist. Why wouldn't you chain yourself to it? Besides, if you don't sign, I'm feeding all three of you to the zombie lions. *Then* I'll send the lions up to Madame Bogbrush's awful school to tuck into your classmates. My lions are always hungry."

Walloping whimpered behind me.

Even Clot stopped singing.

"You have until the interval to make your choice. I trust it will be the right one," said the Ring Mistress. She stalked away without looking back.

That was that.

I'd failed.

I'd let everyone down.

And now, if we didn't join the circus forever, we were going to be eaten.

Walloping shook the bars …

… and pushed the bars …

… and pulled the bars.

"I is strong! The bars should bend. Why isn't they bending?" he said. A giant blob of sweat plopped down his cheek and splashed onto the floor.

I squeezed over to the old wooden chest that was in the cage with us. Inside, it glowed with piles of papers, with perfect fang marks in the corners.

"The Never-Ending Contracts are all here. Why would the Ring Mistress leave them with us?" I wondered aloud.

Walloping thudded to the floor, crossing his legs and rubbing his jaw. "Because she doesn't think we is ever getting out," he moaned, blowing his nose into his sleeve. "We can't stays in here forever! I is hungry and I needs a wee!"

"I don't know what you two are looking so glum about!" said Clot. "I'm a dentist's apprentice. Making things open wide is my speciality! Now then, what do we need?" Clot flapped her cloak and pulled out an assortment of silver pointy tools with bendy bits, jabby bits and extra-pointy bits.

I'd seen loads of people picking locks on Small TV shows. It was easy. "That one!" I said, choosing Clot's pointiest toothpick and poking it into the rusty lock. "I'll have us out in a jiffy!"

...

...

...

Several jiffys later ...

"*Doo bee doo bee dee, we're lock picking, yippee!*" sang Clot. But lock picking was harder than it looked. Clot took the toothpick from me and gave it a good wiggle. She'd get us out.

...

...

Even more jiffys later ...

"Why isn't it working?" I said, panic spilling over me faster than a vampire dentist's mouthwash.

"Maybe the lock is scared of dentists," said Clot, dropping the toothpick.

There had to be another way. I looked through the bars, hoping for a flash of inspiration. Instead, I saw a blinding flash … of gold glitter!

You'll never guess who was outside the cage …

"Norma!" cried Walloping. "Oh boy is I happy to see you! Has you got any sandwiches?"

Norma Enormous was dressed top to toe in glitter and sparkles. Every bit of her shimmered and jingled. Every bit apart from the glowing green light that wound round her wrist and snaked towards my cloak pocket. She was still chained to her contract.

"What? It's my show costume," said Norma, seeing the gawp on my face.

"You're actually taking part?" I said, horrified. "You can't let the Ring Mistress win! We're here to rescue you!" I knew Norma liked being star of the show, but not for a zombie-filled child-stealing circus that was threatening to eat all her classmates.

Norma shook her head. "I think you'll find I'M rescuing YOU," she said, waving a key at me. "Stole

167

these from the Ring Mistress when she was busy bossing around the zombie clowns. When the light on my wrist got brighter, I figured you were finally on your way." Her wrist glowed like a green laser beam now. "If you hadn't run off with my contract, I'd have been out ages ago," she said, clicking the key in the lock.

Clot, Walloping and me tumbled out the cage. Walloping uncrossed his legs and dashed into the nearest bushes.

"Naturally, I did my own research while you were off with the d-d-dentists." Norma's face paled as she looked at Clot. "I think a vampire bit the contracts. And I think the massive mirror in the dressing-room tent could reverse it."

"That's what I said!" I said, dusting myself off.

"*Rurooogha!*" trumpeted Twinkle behind us.

"*Wahwoooool!*" howled Luna, beside her.

"*Squawk!*" squawked Fruity, flapping around Clot's head.

Everyone was making FAR too much noise!

"Quick!" said Norma, looking over her shoulder. "Grab as many contracts as you can and follow me. The mirror's this way!"

"The Lost Narcissus!" said Clot, clapping her hands as we ran after Norma. "It's the vampires' stolen mirror! I know it."

We zig-zagged around caravans, tents and mouldy floss stalls until we came to a green velvet tent with a fancy sign outside that said *Dressing Room*. Swirls of glitter blew around it.

A zombie clown stood at the entrance, munching a slime toffee apple. He saw Norma and snarled. "You should be on stage, not getting dressed." He spat globs of stinking green slime at her. Then, spotting Clot, he backed away. "No dentists backstage," he said, folding his arms.

"Can't she just ..." I began, but the zombie stopped me. "Hey, you're the Small we're feeding to the lions, aren't you?" He grinned a little too widely. The stench from his decaying mouth was so strong my vision swam, and my legs wobbled. "Nice of you to dress up for the occasion. In you go." The clown shoved me into the tent, with Walloping and Norma bounding in behind me.

"Over there," said Norma. She pointed past a bedraggled huddle of grey-faced acrobats and rails full of sparkly leotards to a mirror as big as Walloping.

I looked back at Clot and mouthed "sorry" before following Norma.

"Wow," I said, staring up at the mirror. It stretched to the top of the tent.

I hoped this would be the last time I pulled Norma's contract from my cloak.

"Ready?" I asked.

"Ready!" they replied.

Norma, Walloping and I put our hands on the contract and held it up in front of the mirror.

The paper shook.

"Gets down!" cried Walloping.

And three green thunderbolts burst through the mirror.

They shot straight at us.

Apprentice name: Clot
Project: Fang Finding
Night: three
Results:
- We've found the right fang, I'm certain.
- But I've also run away from school.
- How will I get a good grade for my project if I don't have a teacher to mark it?
- Why am I still writing this?
- Why is the swamp so scared of me?
- And woah, what's that green li⟍

Teeth examined: 1
Matches: 1
Schools run away from: 1

Chapter twenty-three

Fangs!

They say, in moments when you are totally and utterly convinced you're going to die, your whole life flashes before your eyes.

Well, after we waved Norma's Never-Ending Contract in front of the Narcissus mirror, all I saw was Walloping lurching towards me and shouting, "Gets down!"

Next thing I knew, I was flat on the dressing-room floor, surrounded by a thick cloud of green smoke and a little pile of ash.

The glowing green chains around Norma's wrists had vanished.

"I'm free!" cried Norma, waving her arms. "We broke the chains!"

The plan worked! And it should have been amazing. Except …

AHHHHHHHH!

ROARRRRRR!

GRRRRRRRR!

… Moans and wails and growls and roars surrounded us faster than a chasing zombie clown. We had piles of contracts to wave at the mirror, but if we stayed here one second longer, we'd be eaten.

"Hurry! Get outside and get back into the swamp!" I said to my friends, dodging the closest zombie clown.

Leaving the circus wasn't easy.

Rows of zombie clowns, lions, acrobats and jugglers gathered outside the dressing-room tent and marched towards us. A swarm of tooth fairies flitted above their heads. And the Ring Mistress was at the front of the pack.

"You expect to let off great green thunderbolts like that without us noticing? Fools!" laughed the Ring Mistress. She cracked her long whip hard on the ground.

"Get them," she said, letting the lions leap past her.

They gnashed their teeth, dribbling green spit on the ground. The jugglers flung ancient clubs at us. The clowns tossed mouldy custard pies (which Walloping lunged for and gobbled). The fairies pelted us with boiled sweets and gobstoppers.

I held my hands up to the approaching pack of undead performers. "We're here to help you! We're breaking your contracts!" I said. Why were they fighting us?

"Don't come any closer!" warned Norma Enormous. "You might have big teeth, but I'm bigger than you!" She raised a sparkly pink circus boot.

"I wouldn't go breaking their chains if you want to save them," said the Ring Mistress. Her green eyes flashed.

"Why not? I'm the best at chain-breaking," said Norma, confident as ever.

"Because," said the Ring Mistress, "every undead performer will die. For good this time."

The zombies moaned and moved closer.

"What is we going to do?" whispered Walloping as a zombie lion sniffed around his stomping boots.

Maybe getting rid of the zombies for good wasn't such a bad idea.

But ... those zombies were children once. What if the Ring Mistress tricked them into joining the circus, too?

"You're lying," said Norma, standing taller. "I broke my contract and I'm still here."

"That's because you're new. Half of this lot are hundreds of years old." She waved her hand at the grey-faced, glowing circus troupe. "They'll never make it."

So *that's* why the zombie performers didn't want our help. A zombie lion gave my ankles a sniff and snarled. I needed another way to reason with the Ring Mistress. And fast.

"We know what Viscount Bloodsucker did," I said, while staying as still as possible. Any sudden moves and the lion could spring for me. "We know it's his fault, not yours that the performers are stuck here like this."

I don't know what I thought would happen next. What I wasn't expecting was that the Ring Mistress would LAUGH.

She laughed so hard, she tipped her head back and opened her mouth wide. Something white and shiny and pointy glistened in the moonlight.

Fangs!

Chapter twenty-four

BITE Me

The Ring Mistress's fangs twinkled under the eerie green circus lights.

"You're a *vampire?*" said Walloping, Norma and me at the same time. "*You* bit the contracts."

"Of course I am and of course I did. Honestly, you call yourselves gifted. All it took was one little set of false teeth and a pair of stilts to trick the lot of you last term." She laughed again. "I am the greatest vampire to ever stalk these swamps. The other vampires only care about polishing teeth – the fools! Not me. I am the one vampire truly worthy of an audience. So I left the tooth business and went into show business."

I looked at the bedraggled circus tent, with its frayed black and green fabric. I looked at the creaking caravans with paint peeling off them. I wondered when the Ring Mistress last had any kind of audience before tonight.

The Ring Mistress followed my gaze, "Yes, over the years my crowds grew smaller. That's why I needed new blood." Her green eyes twinkled. "Feeding a Small to a zombie lion, that's what swamp goblins call entertainment! I must give my adoring public what it wants."

"*Ruroogha!*" trumpeted Twinkle, still chained to her tree.

"*Wawooool!*" howled Luna beside her.

"*Let's see your teeth!*" pleaded Gargle and Floss from their faraway tree.

"Pah!" said Norma. "You don't have an adoring public!"

"I do now," said the Ring Mistress. "Our Big Top is full for the first time in years. All thanks to you!"

The lions snarled.

Their bones glowed green through their shadowy skin.

They crouched on their hind legs, ready to pounce.

Norma and Walloping were bigger than the lions, but they weren't faster.

I caught Clot's eye. She'd been perched up a swamp tree with Fruity ever since the zombie clown shooed her away. Seeing her up there gave me an idea.

I started hopping …

… and twirling …

… and gnashing my teeth.

Finally, I flashed my blue vampire torch in the air.

Walloping grinned and copied me.

"What are you doing?" said Norma. "This is no time for dancing!"

For once, Norma was wrong. This might be our only way to escape.

Clot jumped from the tree, making Fruity wake with a shriek. They landed in the middle of the circle with us.

The zombie lions leaped back.

A group of decaying acrobats cartwheeled away.

And Clot shone her torch high in the air. "Goody!" she cried, "we'll actually see if the BITE signal works!"

"Pah! Your pathetic torches won't save you now!" said the Ring Mistress. Although I noticed she

looked to the
sky before
shouting at
her scattered
performers, "Get
back here and attack!"

A zombie lion launched at my
chest, knocking me flat on the ground.

Before I could get up, a zombie clown charged for
me and …

… *SPLAT!* They threw an algae and custard pie at
my face.

"Uh uh! Don't eat the Small yet! Get him to the

main stage. The swamp goblins will LOVE this!" said the Ring Mistress.

I coughed and spluttered and kicked, but I was no match for a zombie lion.

"Oww! Gerrof me!" Neither was Walloping. He thudded to the ground beside me, grabbing his jaw. I heard the high-pitched giggle of a swarm of tooth fairies above us, followed by another snarl and yelp.

"Eek!" I cried. A zombie lion dragged me by the scruff of my neck towards the Big Top.

Flying hoops and flaming clubs crashed by my ears and flew past my nose. Norma and Clot tried to chase after me, but they couldn't dodge the flaming juggling clubs fast enough.

The zombie lion's breath was colder than all the snow and ice on the Jaw Mountains. I gasped and kicked and twisted and wriggled. The lion yelped, but didn't let go.

"*Ruroogha!*" trumpeted Twinkle.

"*Wawhoooool!*" howled Luna.

"*Show us your gnashers!*" cried Gargle and Floss.

"*Hissss*" hissed the swamp goblins inside the Big Top tent. "*Yesssss! Yessssss! Thissssss issss the show we was promisssssssed!"* They wiggled their cat-like ears in approval and beat their wings in eery applause.

"That's right!" boomed the Ring Mistress, bowing towards the swamp goblin crowds. "Behold, the wonderful, spectacular, unspeakable sight … of a Small being eaten live on stage!"

"Yessssss! Yessssss!" squealed the swamp goblins.

No. No! I thought. This couldn't be how it ends. Could it?

"Walloping! Norma! Clot!" I cried.

No reply. I was in a Big Top full of swamp goblins, but I'd never felt more alone.

CLANK

"Ruroogha!"

"Twinkle?" I heard the skelephant's chains rattle outside the tent. Poor Twinkle. Who would save her now?

"Ruroogha!" she trumpeted again.

"Wawoool!" Luna howled.

"Open wider!" shouted Gargle and Floss.

The spikey, raspberry-blowing, can-can-dancing, cymbal-crashing worry monster in my tummy giggled and curtsied. Her work was done.

182

Deep down, I always knew it. I wasn't the Chosen One. I was just a boy.

A boy who was about to be eaten.

"Dinner time!" boomed the Ring Mistress, laughing in delight.

And everything went black.

Chapter twenty-five

Blood Relatives

No, I wasn't dead.

Everything wasn't *that* kind of black.

"*Rurooogha!!!!*"

It was the kind of black you only get when your best skelephant friend crashes through an Unspeakable Big Top, dragging an entire swamp tree behind them ...

"*Wawooool!*"

... Just as a pack of werewolves in human form sprint into that same Big Top, waving clubs, shaking their fists and growling ...

... And HUNDREDS of fruit bats fly towards you, blocking out the lights. Hundreds of bats carrying hundreds of vampire dentist apprentices – and

dropping
them right
in the middle of
the circus.

"*Dentissssssssts!
Essssssssscape!*"
hissed the swamp goblin
audience, skuttling out
the tent and into the
darkness.

Twinkle had freed
herself to save me! She stomped
and trumpeted at the zombie lion
until its teeth unclenched from my
dungarees and I dropped to the stage with a
thud. The lion yowled and ran away.

I stumbled to my feet and hugged Twinkle hard.
"You saved me!" I cried.

And the BITE signal worked!

The vampires were here, swooshing their
toothbrushes like swords.

Viscount Bloodsucker was first to the stage. He pulled on his blue rubber gloves as he ran. "Never fear! The dentists are here!" he said, flashing a ginormous smile. "What can we help with? A wobbly tooth? A quick polish? We, the Happy Fang dentists are here to serve … oh." Viscount Bloodsucker spotted me on stage with Twinkle. His face soured. "It's you. Another one of your tricks, I suppose?"

The vampire's face soured even more when he clocked where he was. "Apprentices!" he said, flapping his cloak and stalking off stage. "Gather your toothbrushes, we're leaving."

But outside the tent, the apprentices weren't going anywhere.

"Look, a zombie acrobat! In real undead life!" said one apprentice.

"Have you seen this? Open wide!" said another, attempting to jab a toothpick into the jaws of a snarling zombie lion.

"Ooh, that clown's looking so sad! I bet a nice clean would cheer you up!" said a third apprentice, running right up to the zombie clown. He didn't even flinch as an algae pie launched at his head.

"And Gargle and Floss are here!" cried several

apprentices at once, rushing to help free their classmates.

The Ring Mistress cracked her whip. "Brother dear, won't you control your students?" she snapped. Looking at his blackened fangs, she added, "I see you got my gift."

A swarm of tooth fairies giggled above us.

"YOU?" said Viscount Bloodsucker, turning even paler than usual. "You put hair dye in the toothpaste? You ruined my photo? I should have known! Ever since those new apprentices arrived asking questions, I had a feeling in my fangs something wasn't right."

Brother dear?

"You're the Ring Mistress's brother?" I blurted before she could reply. So, Viscount Bloodsucker was helping her all along! He was only being nice to get us in the photograph!

The Ring Mistress marched up to him. "Stop your moaning! You don't like the Small, I loathe the Small, so let's get back to the show and let the zombie lions eat him, okay?" She smiled sweetly at her brother.

"Release Gargle and Floss, and you can do what you like," said Viscount Bloodsucker, turning to leave. "Just don't involve me or my apprentices ever again."

"Wait!" I cried. My heart thudded harder than Walloping's stomping boots. If the vampires left, the zombie lions would still eat us! "The circus performers need you!" I said. I pointed at the zombie lion who'd dragged me into the Big Top a moment before. "The lion yelped when he bit my dungarees. He's got a wobbly front tooth." The lion whimpered at us from behind a caravan.

"Yes!" said Clot, running over, waving a toothbrush. "And that undead acrobat's right cheek is extra puffy. Looks like a tooth infection to me."

The apprentices surrounded the acrobat and cooed.

"Um," said Walloping, stepping forwards. "Actually, Viscount Bloodsucker, I needs help." What was my best friend saying? He was *terrified* of dentists!

"It's my mouth," he said glumly. "Ever since I eats the tooth fairies' tooth ripper toffees, my tooth has been hurting so much. Perhaps you could looks at it?"

That's why he kept holding his jaw! I flung my arms around my best friend's knees. It was the bravest thing he'd ever done.

Viscount Bloodsucker glared at us, not saying a word.

A second later, his face broke into a beaming smile. "Well, apprentices, what are we waiting for? We've got teeth to tend to!"

The tooth fairies raised their fists, but Viscount Bloodsucker swatted them away.

The apprentices gargled in delight, briefly spelling *HOORAY* in the sky with jets of blue mouthwash before coaxing hiding performers out of their caravans and down from the trees.

And the Ring Mistress looked annoyingly ... *happy*.

"The stench!" she cried. "The decay! Why, the inside of my performers' mouths is the most unspeakable thing I've ever seen or sniffed!"

Stinky spit and toothpaste flew everywhere. The air was thick with clouds of putrid bin bag breath puffing from every performer's mouth.

It was also total chaos. Which meant no one would notice Norma, Clot and me slip inside the dressing-room tent.

If we were going to destroy those Never-Ending Contracts and break those glowing green circus chains once and for all, now was the time.

Chapter twenty-six

Twinkle's Last Act

The zombie performers yowled and howled while the apprentices fought to polish their rotting teeth.

"I'll help the vampires," said Clot, waving her toothbrush and toothpicks. "If I look in the Narcissus mirror, I might get stuck staring at myself forever!"

She headed for the closest zombie lion. "Come on kitty, open wide!"

A heavy hand landed on my shoulder. But it wasn't a zombie clown or a vampire. It was a man with hairy arms and a thick hairy beard. His voice was gruff. "We've hunted our Luna's scent ever since the circus took her," he said.

He must be the leader from Luna's werewolf pack! I instinctively took a step back.

"The Unspeakable Circus smells so bad and moves so often, it was impossible to find her," he said, "Until those bats screeched over our den to lead us here. I hear you called them. Thank you."

A band of grizzly were-people surrounded the circus. They growled and pounced on any zombie performer who tried to escape.

"Catch!" said Norma, throwing the Ring Mistress's keys at me. "You can unchain Luna with these."

The were-man and I rushed to Luna's cage.

"Papa Wolf!" she cried, reaching her arms through the bars as we approached.

The second the lock *clicked*, Luna leaped at her father, half-growling, half-sobbing.

Then she sprang at me. "Thank you, thank you, thank you!" she panted.

But the glowing green circus chains still twisted around her wrist.

"I'll reverse your contract. I know how, now." I said, dashing back to the dressing-room tent.

"Wait! I'll help you!" she cried, padding behind me.

Norma, Luna and I sifted through the piles of

contracts, looking for the names of every chained child, bogey, werewolf, and Gargle and Floss.

"Here's mine!" said Luna, pulling a glowing page from near the top of the pile.

I held it up to the mirror (ducking just before the green thunderbolt struck!). A second later, Luna's chains disappeared. She tilted her head back and howled.

"*Wawhooooooool!*"

"*Wahwhoooool!*" came the howls of her pack, who charged into the tent. Papa Wolf was first. He wrapped his hairy arms round his daughter and held on tight until she wriggled away.

"We've got more performers to save!" she panted.

Between us, we unchained bogey children, baby swamp flappers, a three-tailed swamp hopper bunny and Gargle and Floss. The vampires immediately joined the other apprentices, attempting to teach zombie lions how to gargle *If you're happy and you know it, flash a fang!*

Soon every child who'd been chained up was free, laughing and shaking with relief.

All but one.

"*Rurooghaaa!*" Twinkle plodded into the dressing-room tent, kicking her football my way. I kicked it back.

"Don't worry," I said, as she wrapped a friendly trunk around me. "We haven't forgotten about you. Here's your contract." I looked in the mirror and back at Twinkle.

"What's wrong?" said Norma, seeing me hesitate.

"Don't you remember what the Ring Mistress said?" I replied. "Twinkle's half-living,

half-dead. If we break her contract, she dies ... for real this time."

Saying the words out loud made me feel like one of those green thunderbolts had blasted me in the chest.

Reversing Twinkle's contract would KILL her. Not reversing it would chain her to the circus forever. What were we going to do?

"*Ruroogha!*" trumpeted Twinkle, knocking her favourite football towards me again. I kicked it back, forcing down the lump in my throat.

We kicked the ball between us. "What do you think?" I asked her. "Do you want to stay in the circus?" She hung her head low in what I was sure was a "no."

"If we reverse the contract," said Norma, patting Twinkle's side, "she'll be with her family again. It's in Walloping's *Big Book for Explorers*. Ghost elephants never forget their herds."

"Would you like that, Twinkle?" I asked. "To be back with your herd?" I stopped myself saying, "Even if that means you can't play football with me."

"*Ruroogha!*" she trumpeted, glowing brighter and holding her head higher.

I gulped. I knew what she was saying.

It was time.

"I guess this is goodbye," I said, giving my friend one last hug. "Thank you for saving me," I whispered.

Twinkle twinkled brightly.

I held her contract up to the mirror, holding my breath as the green thunderbolt struck.

Whoosh!

That's when the Ring Mistress burst in.

"Twinkle, you stupid beast! Don't leave me! You're a star!" She paused. "I know we haven't had a proper audience in years, but that can change! You should have seen the swamp goblins tonight. They filled the Big Top! We'll get those crowds again, I know it!"

The Ring Mistress put a new contract on the ground by Twinkle's foot. "All you have to do is stamp here and you're mine, forever!"

But the Ring Mistress was one green thunderbolt too late.

Twinkle's shimmery body slumped and faded to the floor, missing the contract by millimetres. Norma put a heavy arm round me. And the air filled with the sound of thundering feet.

I gasped.

A herd of ghostly white elephants charged towards us.

And a wisp of white cloud came off Twinkle's body, like steam on hot buttered toast. The cloud was unmistakably Twinkle-shaped.

I held my hand out to stroke her. It passed straight through.

Ghost-Twinkle flapped her ears.

"Goodbye, Twinkle," I whispered, forcing a bright smile. "I'll never forget you."

Twinkle turned and charged through the sky.

She was gone.

All that was left was her favourite football.

"Hey, that's a nice ball," said Luna, moving beside me. She gave Twinkle's football the lightest flick with her right toe and balanced the ball on her head.

"You like football?" I said, with a hint of a smile. My giant classmates had tried to play, but their big feet kicked the ball miles with every touch.

"Of course I do," she grinned. "Maybe we can play later … after …" She gestured to the piles of contracts.

"Gah! Get away from my mirror, you wretched children!" said the Ring Mistress, cracking her whip so hard it made me jump. "You'll pay for losing my star act, you mark my words."

Every Never-Ending Contract we had left belonged to a zombie performer.

The Ring Mistress barged past me, gathering as many of them as she could. Which wasn't many as Norma sat on the pile.

"Bloodsucker!" cried the Ring Mistress. "Bloodsucker, get in here!"

The vampire swooshed in, covered in toothpaste, zombie spit ... and his biggest grin yet. When he saw the mirror, he held his hand to his heart.

"The Narcissus!" he gasped, straightening his cloak and wiping away the toothpaste. "How I've missed you!" He gazed into the glass.

"Please, brother dear! You wouldn't destroy your only sister's only circus, would you?" said the Ring Mistress. She fell to her knees, tugging on the ends of the Viscount's cloak.

Viscount Bloodsucker kept staring at himself. He tilted his head one way, then the other. "Beautiful," he murmured.

I could see why Clot kept away from mirrors. The Viscount wasn't listening to a word the Ring Mistress said.

"Wowee!" gasped Walloping, running into the tent. His lip was double the size and his mouth was even more dribbly than usual. Now he'd seen the dentist, I hoped his tooth would stop hurting soon.

"De apprendices dis do happy," he struggled to say. "And oh boy, my tooth does feel so much better. Maybe these dentists isn't all bads!"

The zombie lion Clot treated wasn't snarling half as much, either.

It gave me an idea.

A horrible idea.

An *unspeakably* horrible idea.

Chapter twenty-seven

Brush with Fame

Viscount Bloodsucker's eyes were almost as wide as his smile (which he was still practising in front of the Narcissus mirror).

"Dentistry ... on stage?" he said, clapping his hands. "This might be even better than putting our school photo on a poster! Do you think swamp creatures would really attend such a glorious event ... to see me?" He twirled and bowed at his reflection, looking positively giddy.

"Yes! Yes!" said the Ring Mistress, crawling towards me. "Sweet child, so full of good ideas! I've always said so."

Huh? I wasn't doing this for her. I was doing it

for every creature with a rotten or painful or wobbly tooth … which I was beginning to think was most of them.

I pushed myself between the Viscount and the mirror. He couldn't stand there admiring himself, we had a show to prepare!

The dreamy look in the Viscount's eyes faded. He blinked hard and finally focussed on me. "We've got plenty of cavity-filled zombie clowns left. We can start with them!" he said. The Viscount led us outside, with only one longing glance back at the mirror.

"Yippee!" cried the apprentices, hearing the plan. They waved their toothbrushes high and ducked every custard and algae pie the zombie clowns pelted at them.

The Ring Mistress cracked her whip. "Don't you worry about the clowns. I'll get them to behave. I am the greatest Ring Mistress the swamp has ever seen!" she said.

"No," said Viscount Bloodsucker. "These are my patients now."

I whispered the next part of my idea in the vampire's ear. He smiled and nodded. "Don't worry, little sister. We have just the job for you."

Crowds of swamp goblins, werewolves, bogeys and giants gathered outside the Big Top.

"I carried invitations across the swamp!" panted Luna, rolling Twinkle's football between her shoulders.

"And we shouted as loudly as we could!" said Norma and Walloping.

"I even convinces the Moaning Marshes to moan about it!" Walloping added.

"Great!" I said. No wonder the Big Top was crammed full, with every creature from the swamp. Well, every creature *apart* from the tooth fairies.

"There's no business like show business, like no business I know!" sang Clot at the top of her voice. "I can't believe I've seen the dawn *and* the bright lights of the stage. The swamp is so much more colourful and wonderful than I ever imagined!"

Fruity flapped in circles around Clot's head. She was excited, too.

"Are we ready?" asked Viscount Bloodsucker.

I took a breath. "I think so."

I stepped onto the stage.

The crowd roared.

"H-h-hello, swamp creatures!" I began, forcing my voice to be louder than a squeak. "Welcome to the most terrifying, most exciting and cleanest performance in the swamp. Show Me Your Gnashers!!"

The crowd shrieked and squealed with delight. Some creatures covered their eyes, like it was too scary to watch.

"Give a big hand, paw, wing or flapper to ... Viscount Bloodsucker!"

The Viscount swept onto the stage amidst gasps and shrieks from the crowd. He took an elaborate bow before lowering his goggles and snapping rubber gloves onto his hands.

"I welcome our first patient!" he said. "Harvey Small!"

The shrieks grew as I opened wide and let the vampire do his best brushing. Whiffs of peppermint wafted through the tent, making the audience splutter.

Cleaning my teeth was the easy bit. I knew what the audience really wanted to see. Walloping and Norma waited in the wings. "Bring on the zombie clown!" I called to them, amidst cheers and screams.

The quivering clown stumbled onto the stage. He

blinked in surprise at the sight of such crowds. He even managed a tiny wave.

"Open wide!" said the Viscount, clearly enjoying the moment. The audience howled at the sight of the zombie clown's stinking, rotten teeth.

Spit flew everywhere.

The clown wriggled.

The audience hid behind their paws, wings and giant hands.

"It's horrible, but I can't take my eyes off it!" shouted Lumbering Turnip from the crowd.

When the zombie's greying teeth were suddenly a gleaming, minty white, everyone gasped.

"How did he do it?" said a bogeyman.

"It must be magic!" said a werewolf.

"**I WANT TO SEE IT AGAIN!**" said Madame Bogbrush, blowing half the audience off their seats as she peered in from the back of the tent. Not even the Big Top was big enough for the Headteacher.

"Again!" shouted the crowd.

"More!"

"What an unusual performance!" said Mum and Dad from their seats in the front row. They were wearing home-made badges that said *My son's a Chosen One.* Somehow, they clapped louder than all the other swamp creatures put together.

"Show us how it's done!" cried the crowd.

I looked at Clot and gave her a big thumbs up. She twirled onto the stage. "If you make an appointment with Happy Fang, we can show you all! Or come back for our next gnasher-brushing performance tomorrow!" she said.

The swamp creatures cooed and flapped and cheered.

"Look! They're not scared of me!" whispered Clot, giving me her biggest beam yet.

And the Ring Mistress? Oh, she had a part to play too. But instead of wearing her fancy red jacket or cracking her whip, she wore white overalls and carried a mop. She shuffled behind her brother, mopping zombie spit from the stage floor.

"You missed a bit, sister dear," said the Viscount, directing her towards a slimy green puddle.

The Ring Mistress muttered something rude under her breath but kept mopping. I grimaced. Some people will do anything to be on stage.

Apprentice name: Clot

Project: Fang Finding

Night: four

What I learned in this project:

1. How to find and identify a vampire fang.
2. That I should keep my best socks away from mirrors.
3. The dawn is worth waiting for.
4. I am not a lone vampire.

Teeth examined: 1

Matches: 1

Friends made: 2

Fangtastic work, young Clot! Ten blood oranges for you when we get back to school. I'm sorry I made this project so hard. Sometimes it's scary admitting who you really are, even when you're a grown vampire like me. Thank you for showing me how to invite swamp creatures in. VB

Chapter twenty-eight

The Not-So-Stinking Swamp

The air in the swamp was fresher. In some places, it was almost as minty as Viscount Bloodsucker's school.

I was happy to be back with my giant classmates. But one thing still bothered me.

"What is it best friend? You has been looking as glum as Clot before she sees the dawn," said Walloping one morning. We'd just tucked into a giant-sized breakfast. "I hope you cheers up before we invites the werewolves and vampires to watch our grunting display!"

That's right, the giants were really inviting the vampires in … and they weren't even screaming about it. And I'd get a game of football with Luna later!

Still, I sighed a long sigh. I was starting to sound like the old Clot, too.

I looked at my best friend. "It's just, I'm meant to be the Chosen One, but I didn't fix any of the school's problems, not really. Twinkle and you got me to the vampires' school. Clot showed me where to find the fang. The bats led the werewolves back to Luna. Norma got us out the circus cage. And without Twinkle, that zombie lion would have gobbled me for dinner!"

I was pleased everything worked out, but I struggled to shake the idea it wasn't really because of me.

Walloping let out a booming guffaw. "Oh best friend, you is SO silly sometimes!" he said. "You doesn't have to fix everything yourself, you knows. You helps Clot and you is nice to all the vampires, no matter how scary they is, and they chooses to help you. You has already rescued Norma once, so she chooses to rescue you. You is nice to the werewolves and they chooses to tell the whole swamp about our show. And I ..." he gave me a gigantic grin. "I chooses

208

to help you because you is my best friend. I chooses you no matter what."

Maybe he was right. We all need each other.

My best friend slapped me on the back, dunking my head in a bowl of swampweed porridge.

"Oops!" he cried.

I didn't mind. I had porridge on my face, but I also had the best friend ever.

"You know what, Walloping?" I said, grinning back. "I choose you, too."

The end. For now. Probably.

Vampire Surveillance Report: #1241

Tooth Fairy: Bonnie Bonbon

Observations:

Pop my candy! I've never seen queues up the mountain like it. All the swamp's creatures are getting their teeth cleaned. And they leave looking SO HAPPY.

Recommendations:

Maybe Happy Fang isn't so bad. Can we get our teeth cleaned too?

Meanwhile in a sweetshop somewhere in the swamp ...

The Tooth Fairy Queen read Bonnie Bonbon's final report and scowled. "NO, NO, NO, NO, NO. NO. IT WAS BAD ENOUGH THAT PESKY SMALL STOLE OUR RAREST FANG. NOW HE AND HIS FRIENDS ARE STOPPING TEETH FALLING OUT ENTIRELY. CREATURES LOVE GOING TO THE DENTIST NOW."

She punched her tiny fist on the sweetshop counter, making the other fairies flap backwards into jars of jellybeans and lollipops.

"ON MY WINGS, HE WON'T GET AWAY WITH IT. YOU KNOW WHAT THEY SAY, DON'T YOU FAIRIES?"

The fairies giggled, nodded and flapped their wings faster. They knew the answer, but the Tooth Fairy Queen said it anyway.

"**REVENGE IS *SWEET*.**"

About the author

Hannah Moffatt is a creative director at a language and behavioural science consultancy, where she spends her days writing very sensible things for businesses. At night, she escapes into the beautifully bonkers world of middle-grade fiction, where she writes significantly less sensible things for children. Hannah lives in London with her husband and a sombrero-wearing toy hedgehog named Cedric.

Acknowledgements

When I started writing Small! I always hoped there'd be a sequel. So I'm enormously grateful to Mikka for trusting me to take readers into the Stinking Sinking Swamp a second time. To Rory for diving back in and creating illustrations even more hilarious than the last. And to Holly, for another perfect cover.

I'm constantly bowled over by the loveliness of the many reviewers, bloggers, teachers, librarians and booksellers who took Small! under their wing and helped it fly. You're all amazing. I hope you've enjoyed hanging out with Harvey again.

Extra special thanks go to Emma Pullar from Waterstones Ashford for being a GIANT champion of Small! from the start. Not even Madame Bogbrush could shout about my little book as loudly as you.

Along the way, my friends and family have been a bookselling force to be reckoned with. Thanks especially to my brother Nick for being Chief Seller Extraordinaire in Oxford and Mum and Dad for making sure everyone they've ever met has at least one copy. And to friends old and new for buying Small!, posting pics and in some cases (I'm looking at you, Lucy) setting up signing tables at their birthday party. I'm so lucky to have you all in my life.

To the *Can I Call Myself a Real Writer Now?* Twitter group – thanks for cheering me on, keeping me sane and writing such brilliant books for me to enjoy. You're the best.

To Terrie, thank you for being a sounding board, source of inspiration and reaching the dizzying heights of friendship I thought only Walloping Toenail could achieve.

To Nick, for even more love and roast potatoes.

And to Lydia, my superstar agent. None of this would be possible without you.